MW01565405

MASS EFFECT™

President and Publisher
MIKE RICHARDSON

Editor
IAN TUCKER

Assistant Editor
MEGAN WALKER

Designer
SARAH TERRY

Digital Art Technician
ALLYSON HALLER

Special thanks to:
Chris Bain, Director of Business Planning and Development • **Aaryn Flynn**, General Manager
Amanda Klesko, Business Development Specialist • **Cathleen Rootsaert**, Lead Writer
Neil Thompson, Director of Art and Animation • **Derek Watts**, Senior Art Director

Thanks also to the entire BioWare team worldwide.

© 2017 Electronic Arts Inc. EA and the EA logo are trademarks of Electronic Arts Inc. BioWare, the BioWare logo and Mass Effect are trademarks of EA International (Studio and Publishing) Ltd. Dark Horse Books® and the Dark Horse logo are registered trademarks of Dark Horse Comics, Inc. All rights reserved. No portion of this publication may be reproduced or transmitted, in any form or by any means, without the express written permission of Dark Horse Comics, Inc. Names, characters, places, and incidents featured in this publication either are the product of the author's imagination or are used fictitiously. Any resemblance to actual persons (living or dead), events, institutions, or locales, without satiric intent, is coincidental.

Published by Dark Horse Books
A division of Dark Horse Comics, Inc.
10956 SE Main Street | Milwaukie, OR 97222

DarkHorse.com

To find a comics shop in your area, call the Comic Shop Locator Service toll-free at (888) 266-4226.
International Licensing: (503) 905-2377

Neil Hankerson Executive Vice President • Tom Weddle Chief Financial Officer • Randy Stradley Vice President of Publishing • Matt Parkinson Vice President of Marketing • David Scroggy Vice President of Product Development Dale LaFountain Vice President of Information Technology • Cara Niece Vice President of Production and Scheduling Nick McWhorter Vice President of Media Licensing • Mark Bernardi Vice President of Digital and Book Trade Sales Ken Lizzi General Counsel • Dave Marshall Editor in Chief • Davey Estrada Editorial Director • Scott Allie Executive Senior Editor • Chris Warner Senior Books Editor • Cary Grazzini Director of Specialty Projects • Lia Ribacchi Art Director • Vanessa Todd Director of Print Purchasing • Matt Dryer Director of Digital Art and Prepress • Sarah Robertson Director of Product Sales • Michael Gombos Director of International Publishing and Licensing

First edition: March 2017
ISBN 978-1-50670-287-2

1 3 5 7 9 10 8 6 4 2
Printed in the United States of America

MASS EFFECT
ADULT COLORING BOOK

With Illustrations by

JUANN CABAL

RON CHAN

GABRIEL GUZMÁN

ANDRES PONCE

MARTÍN TÚNICA

Dark Horse Books

"Well, let me know if you want me to get them on the channel and then hang up on them. You know, for old times' sake."
—Jeff "Joker" Moreau

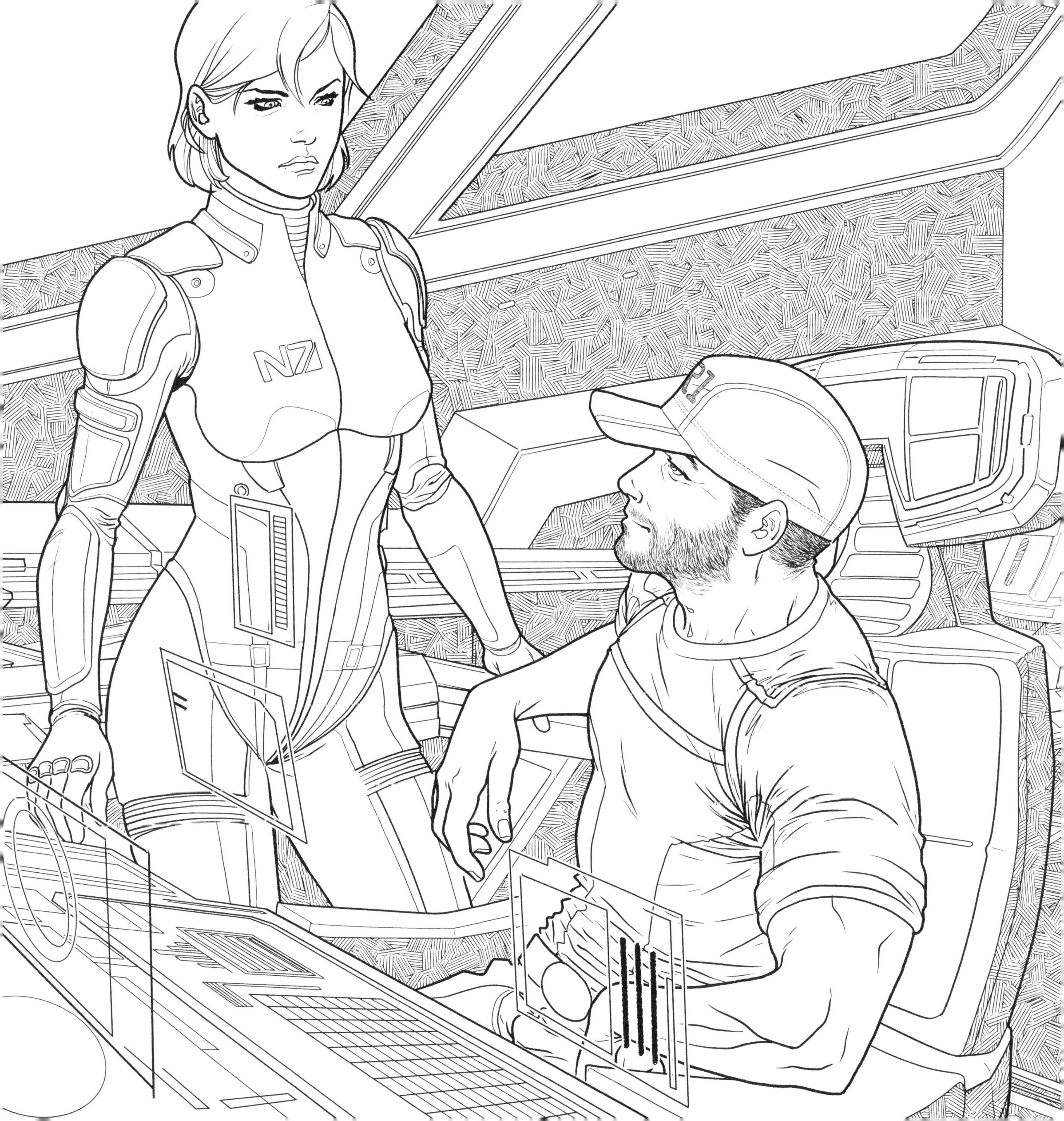
N7

"It's always a good idea to RTFM, ma'am."
—Kaidan Alenko

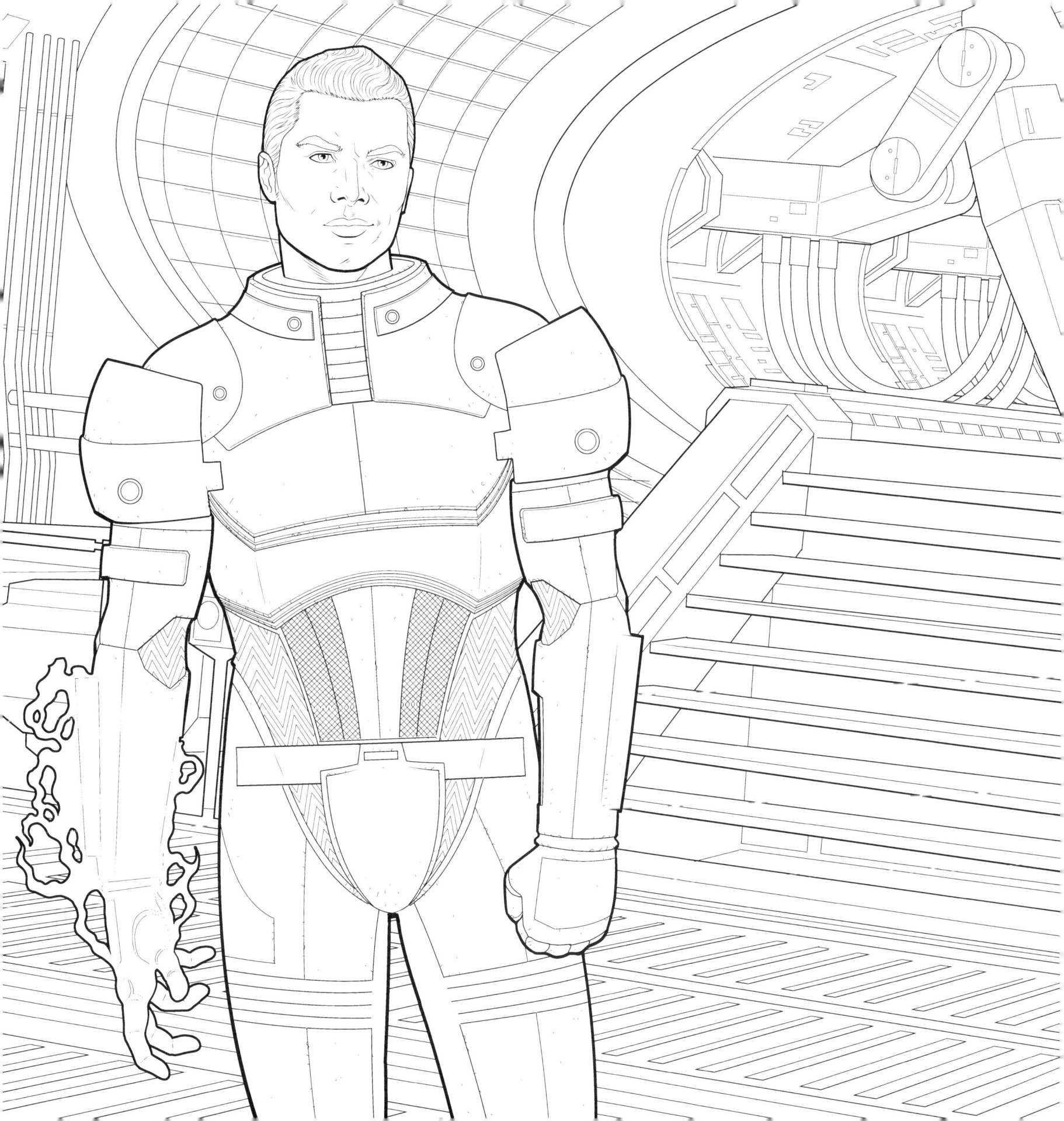

"Why is it whenever someone says, 'With all due respect,' they really mean, 'Kiss my ass'?"
—Ashley Williams

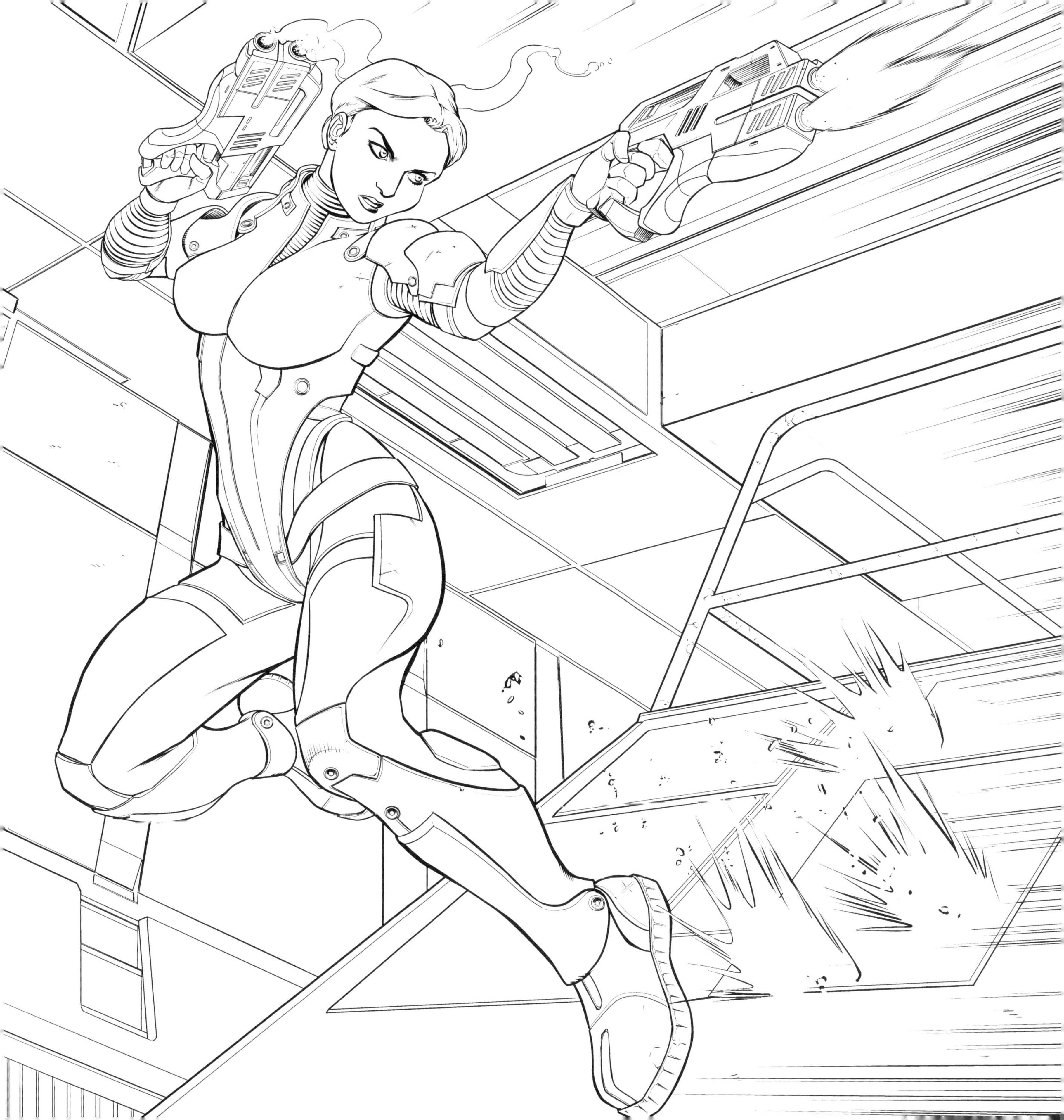

"Why do people always assume we enjoy putting ourselves in harm's way?"
—Garrus Vakarian

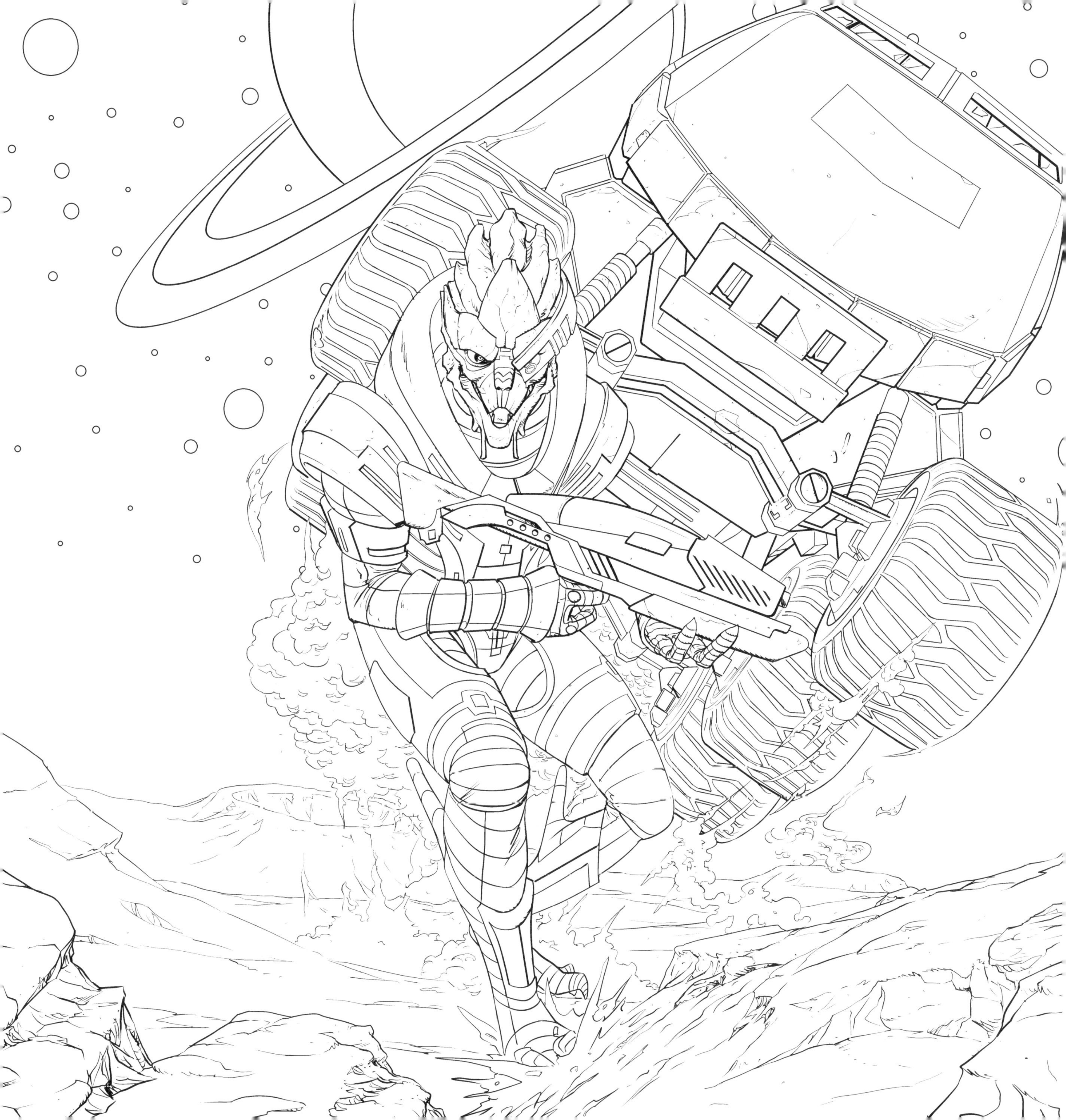

"There is something compelling about you, Shepard."
—Liara T'Soni

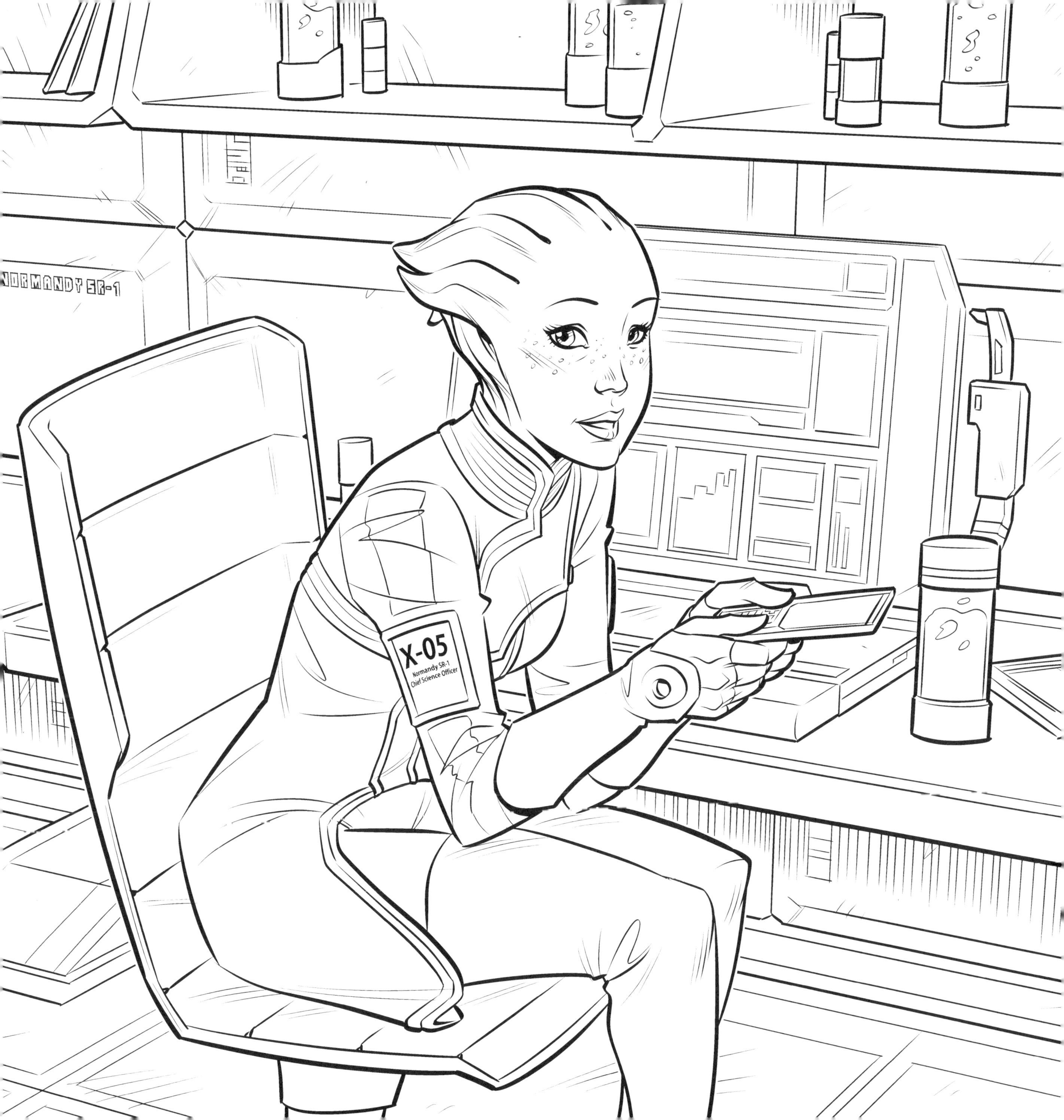
NORMANDY SR-1
X-05
Normandy SR-1
Chief Science Officer

"Takes me back to the old days. Us against the unknown, killing it with big guns. Good times."
—Urdnot Wrex

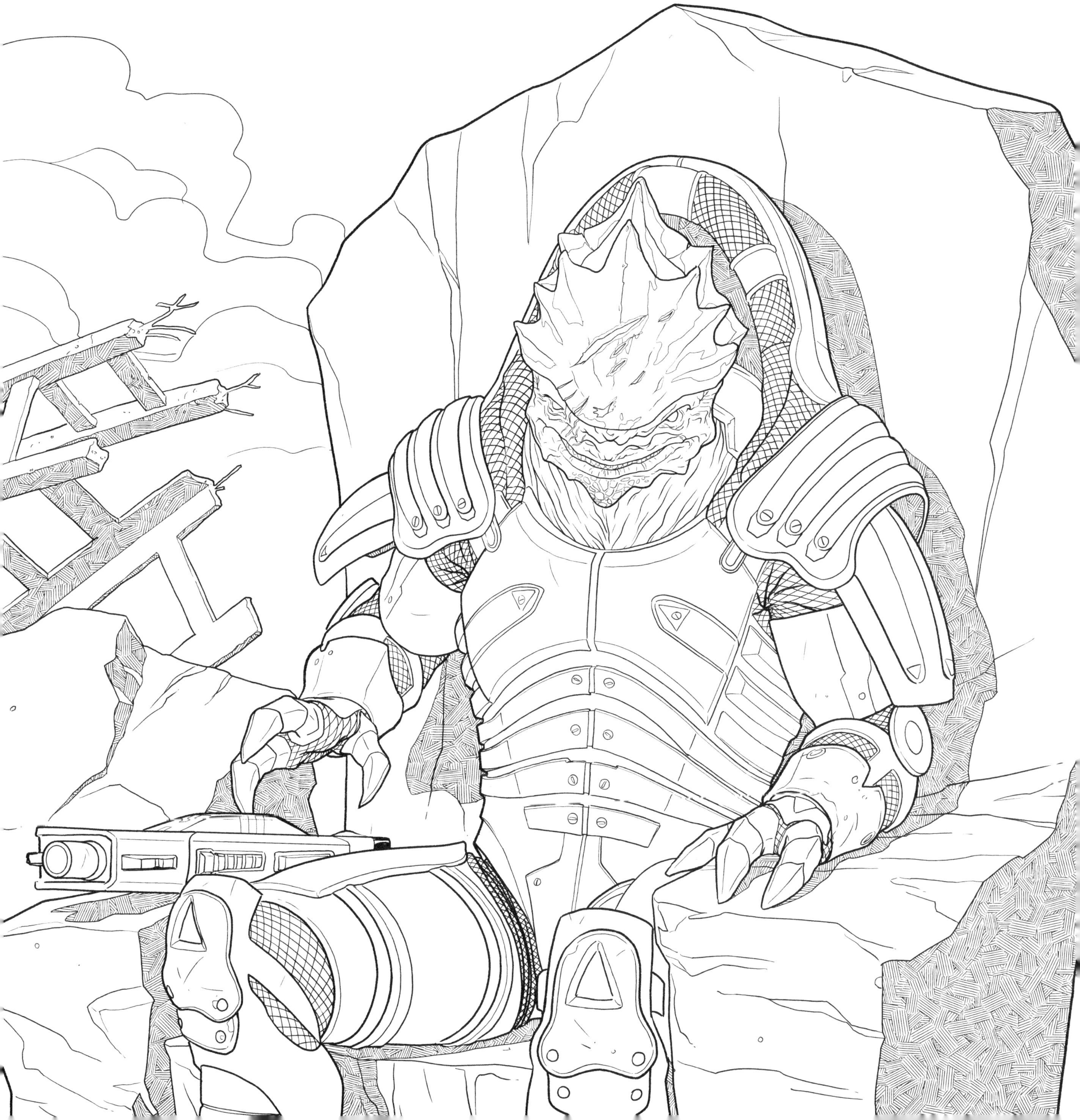

"Is submission not preferable to extinction?"
—Saren Arterius

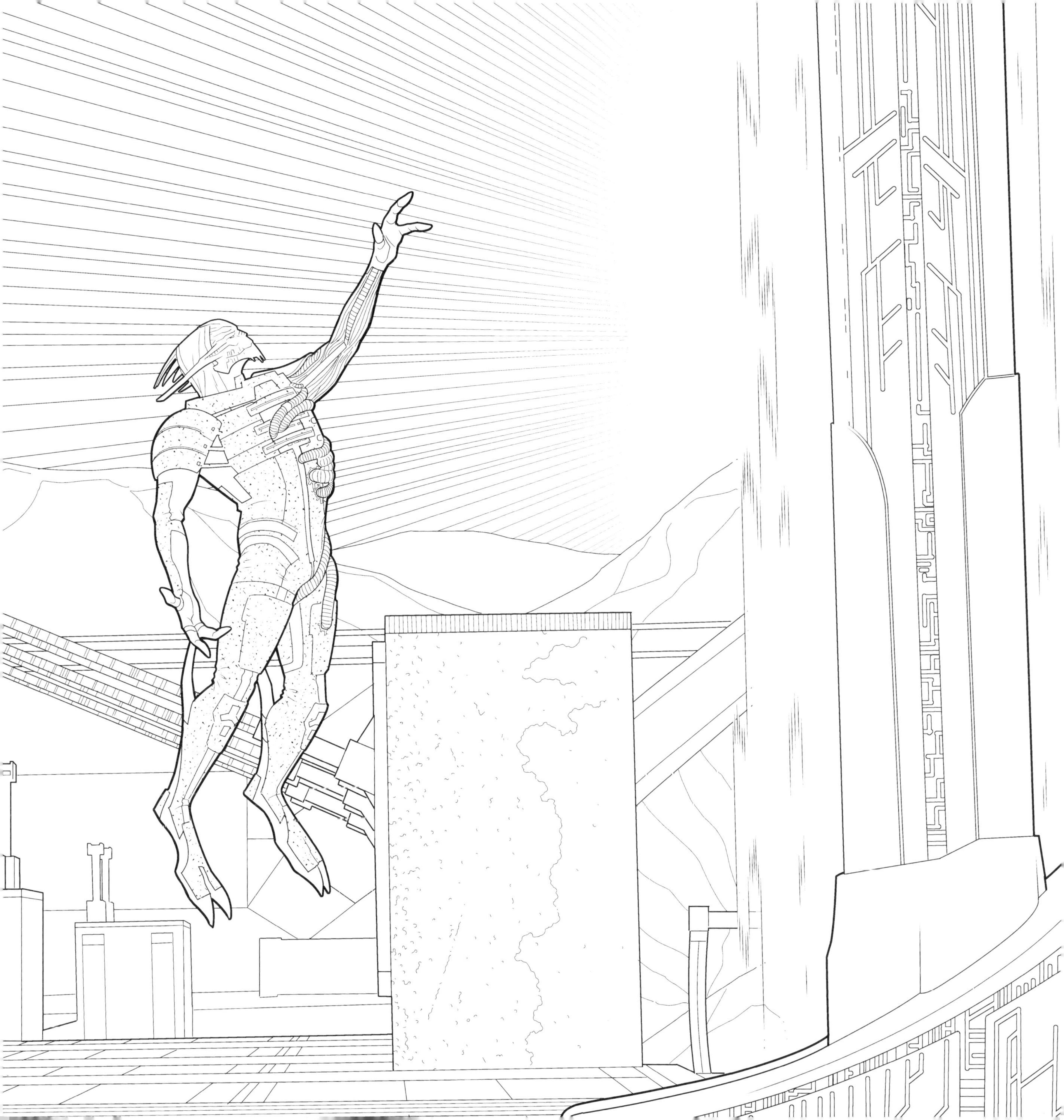

"Yes, it's a pity that most of the technology I had planned to bring back to the Flotilla has subsequently tried to kill us."
—Tali'Zorah nar Rayya

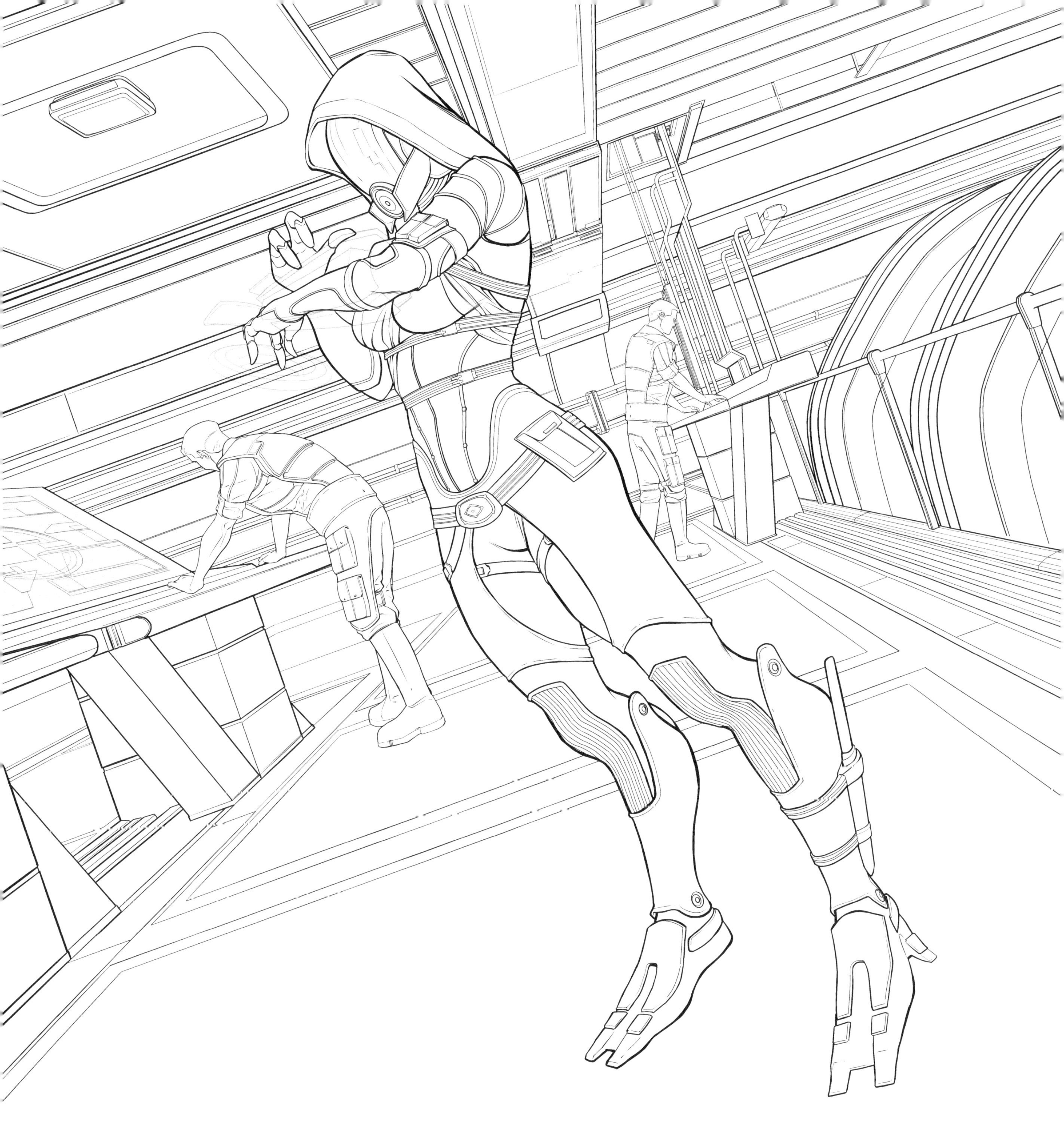

"Put the *Normandy* in my hands and I'll make her dance for you..."

—Jeff "Joker" Moreau

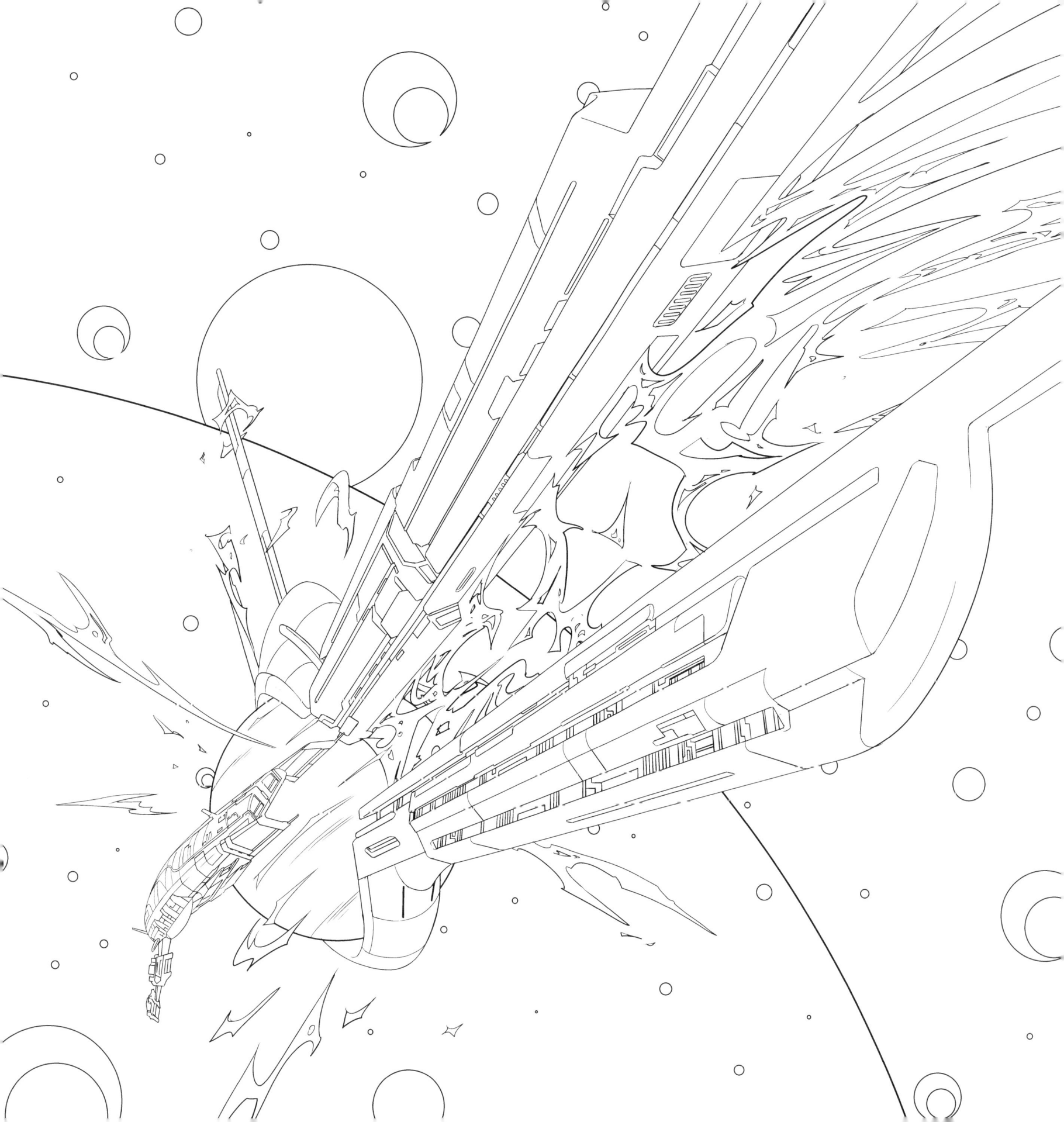

"Commander. Any word on my missing men?"
"I found them. What was left of them. They ran into a thresher maw."
—Rear Admiral Kahoku
and Commander Shepard

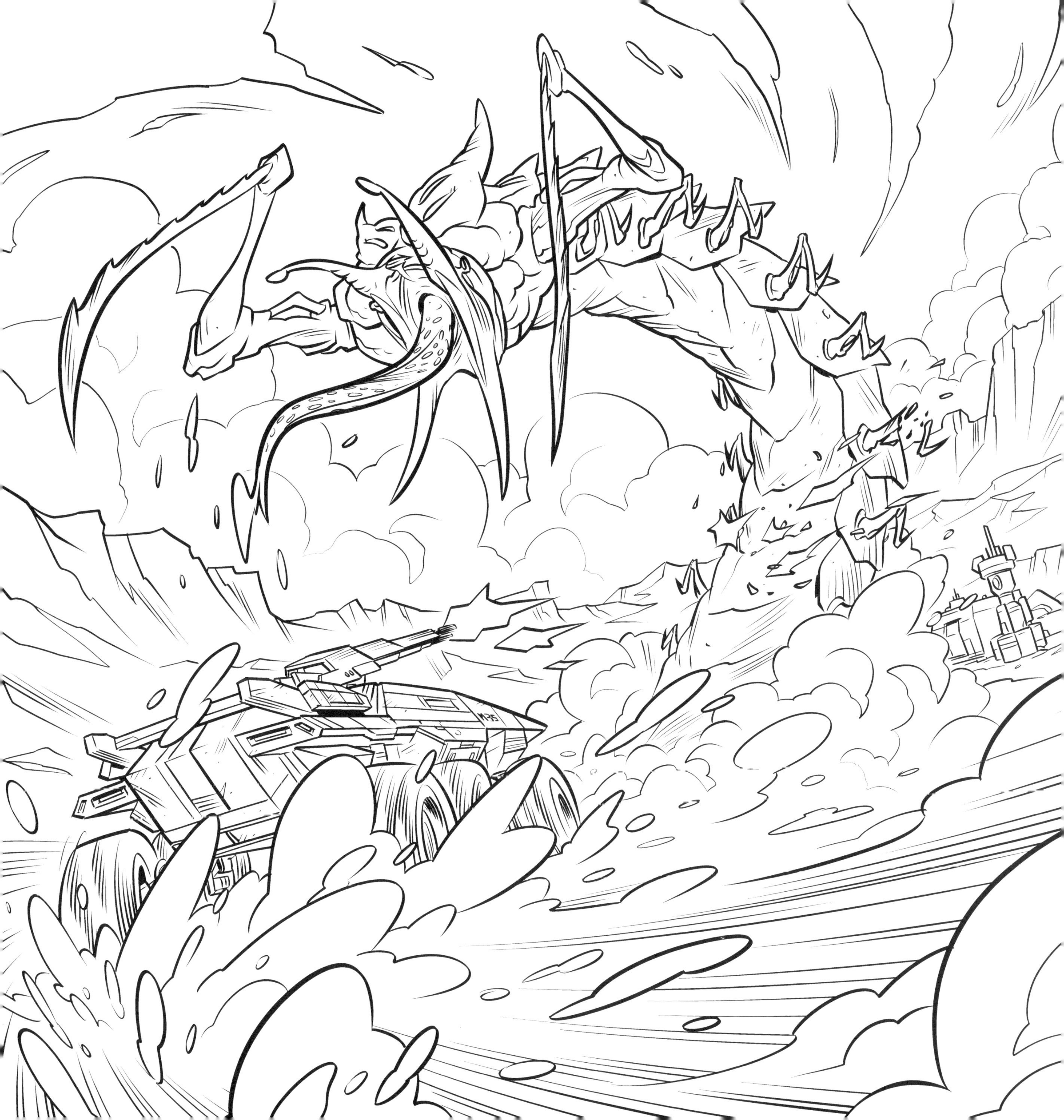
M35

"The geth killed billions and forced us from our homeworld. Most quarians believe we have paid properly for our mistake."
—Tali'Zorah nar Rayya

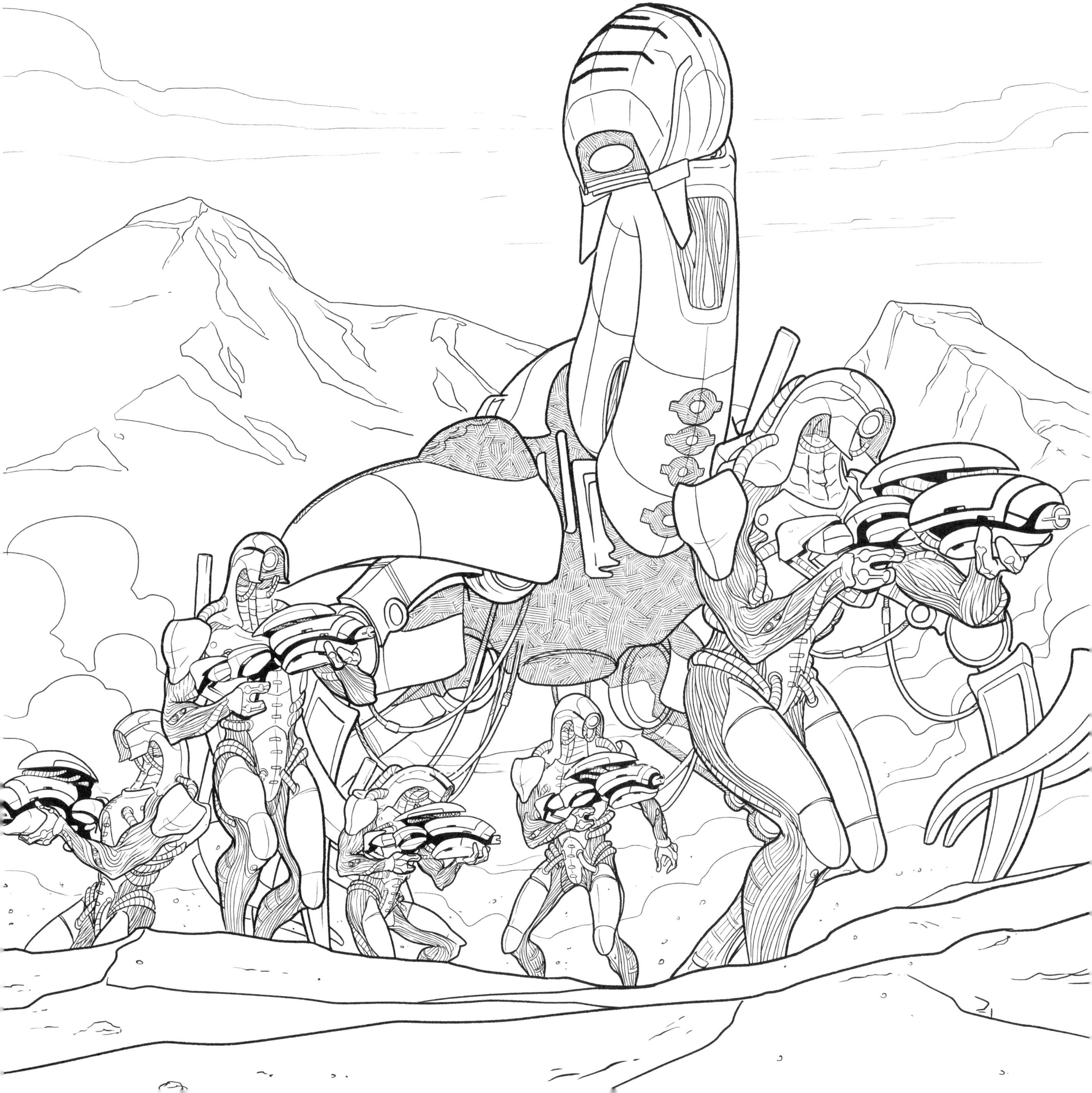

"We impose order on the chaos of organic evolution. You exist because we allow it, and you will end because we demand it."
— *Sovereign*

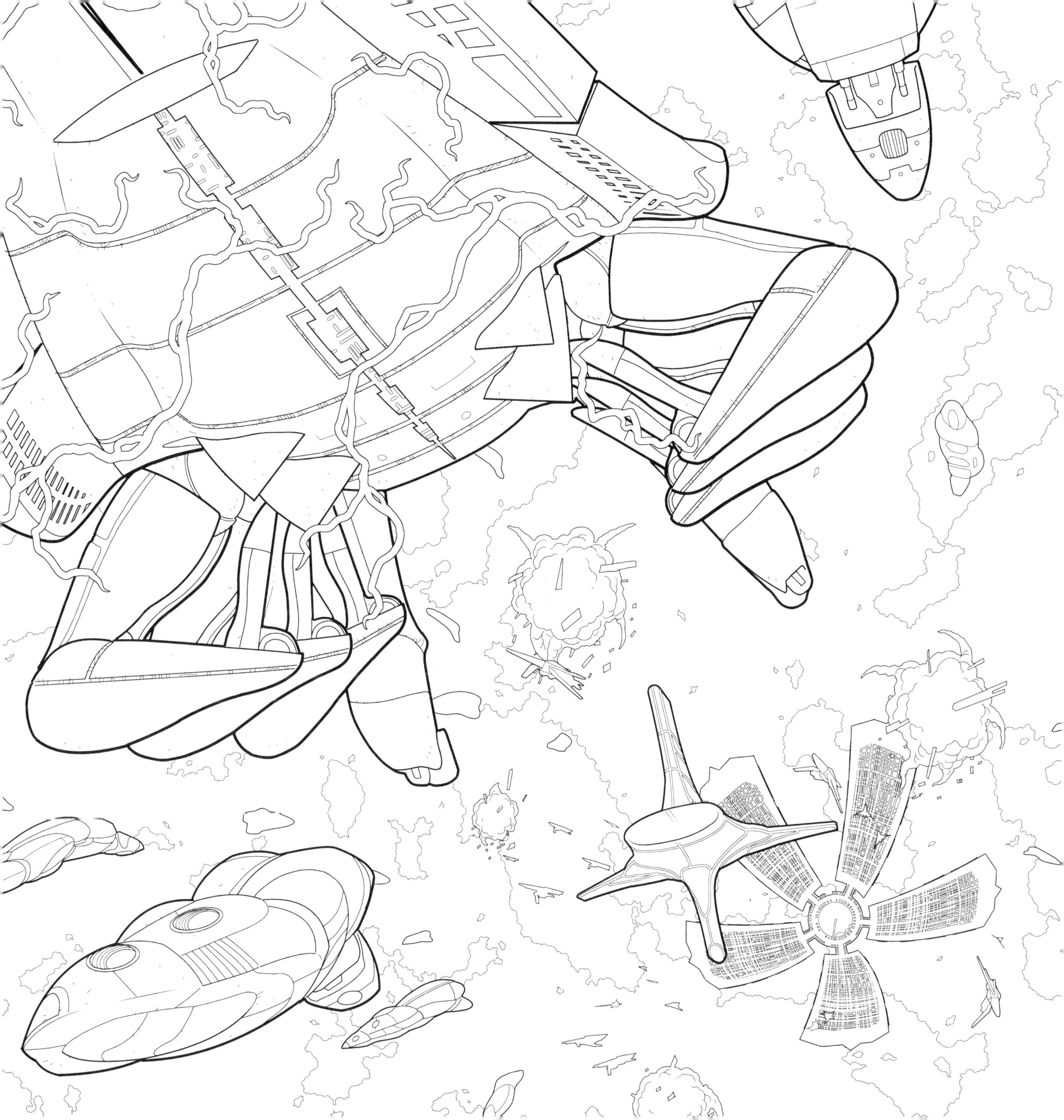

"Salvation comes with a cost. Judge us not by our means, but what we seek to accomplish."
—The Illusive Man

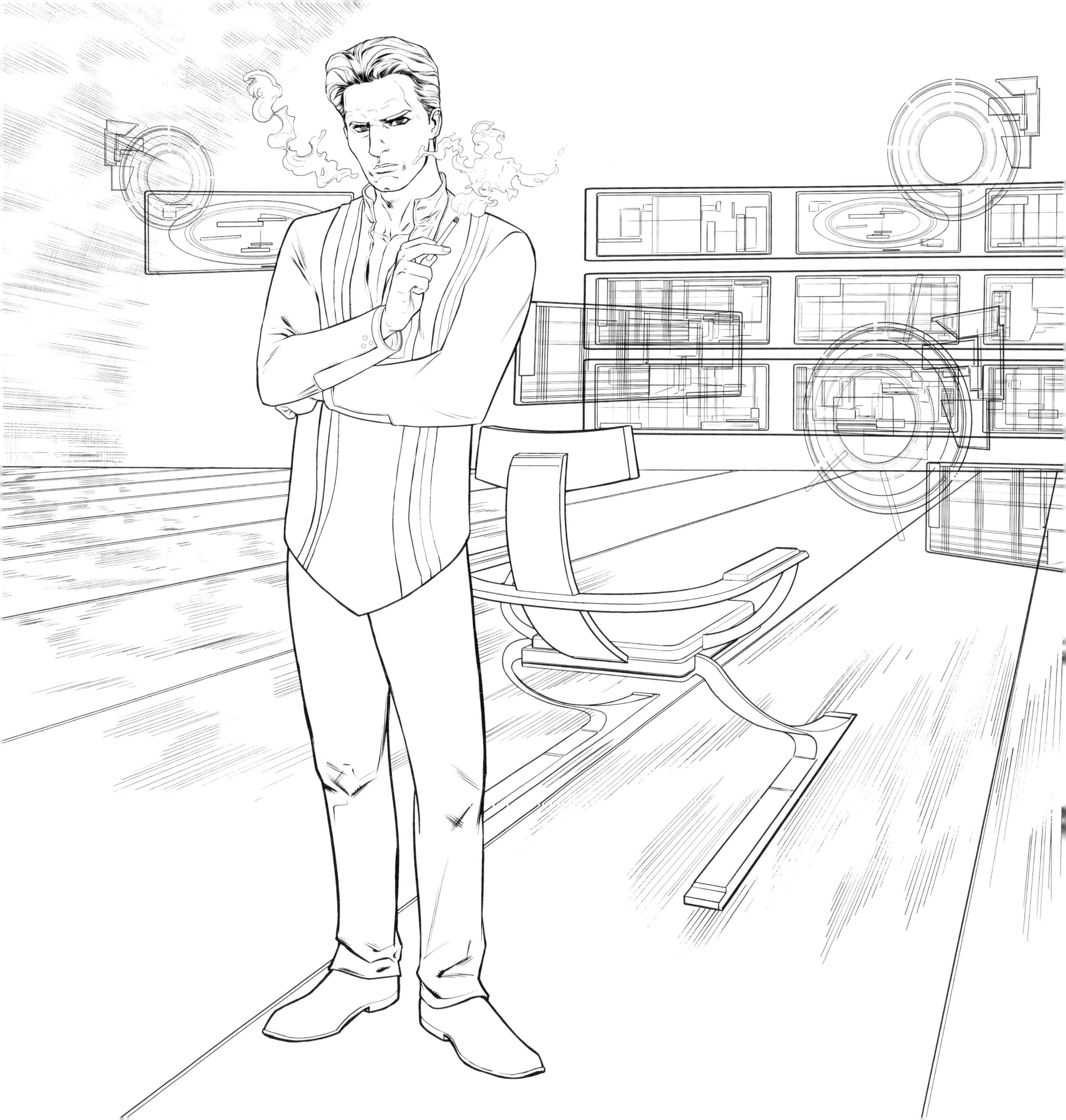

"If we live, we'll get loud and spill some drinks on the Citadel."
—Jacob Taylor

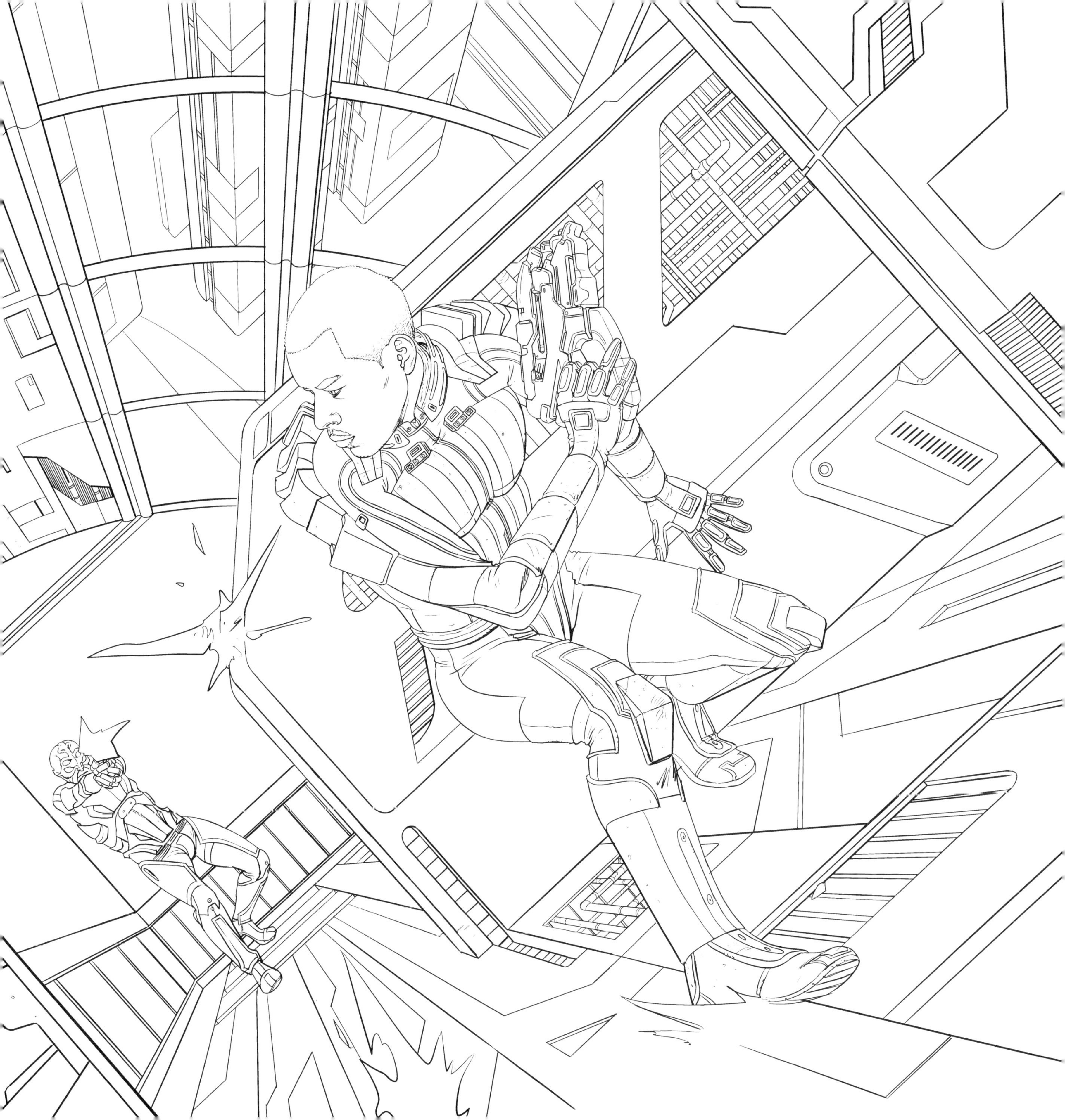

"Worried about my qualifications? I can crush a mech with my biotics or shoot its head off at a hundred yards. Take your pick."
—Miranda Lawson

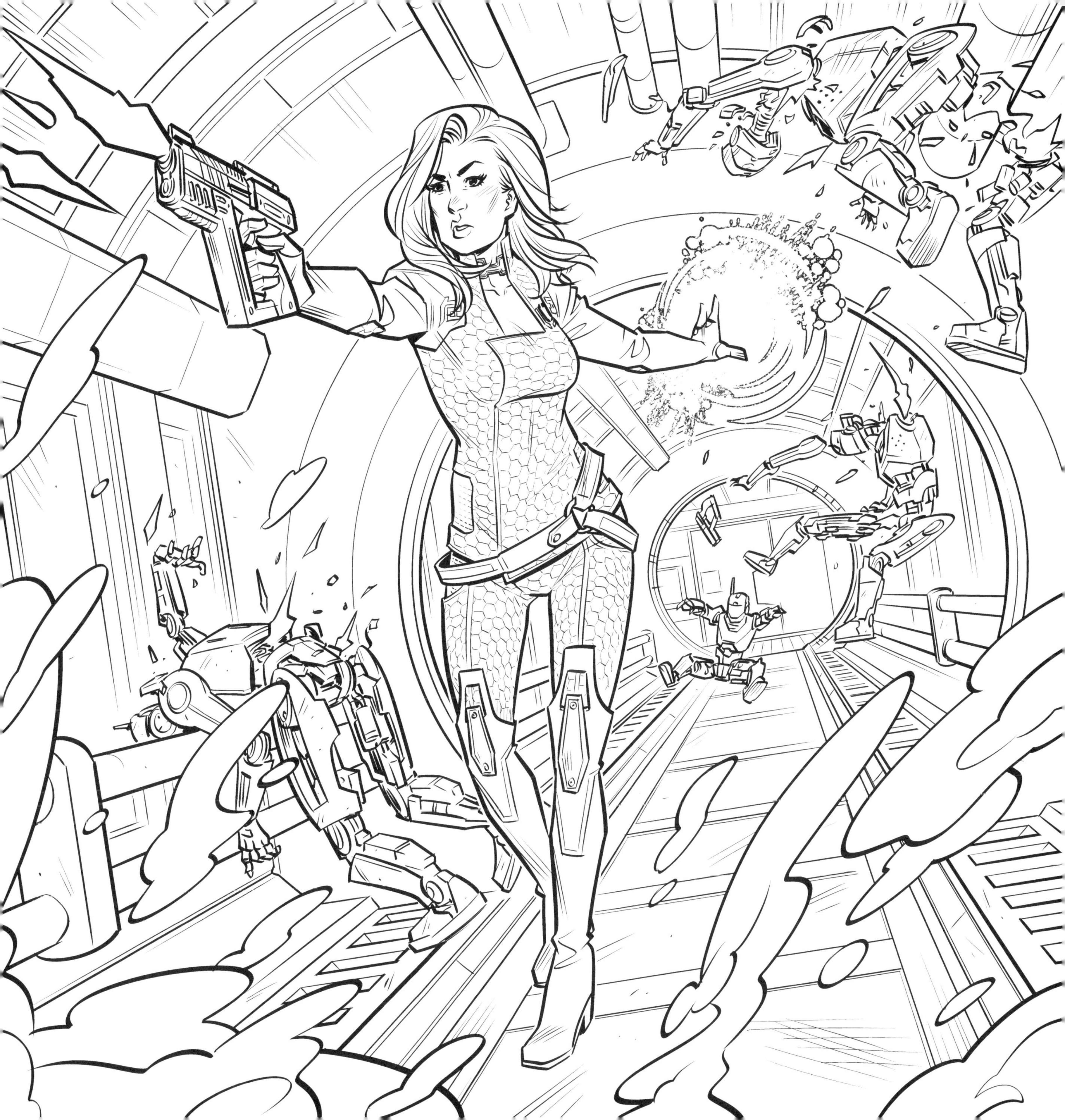

"I am the very model of a scientist salarian.
I've studied species turian, asari, and batarian.
I'm quite good at genetics (as a subset of biology),
because I am an expert (which I know is a tautology).
My xenoscience studies range from urban to agrarian.
I am the very model of a scientist salarian."
—Mordin Solus

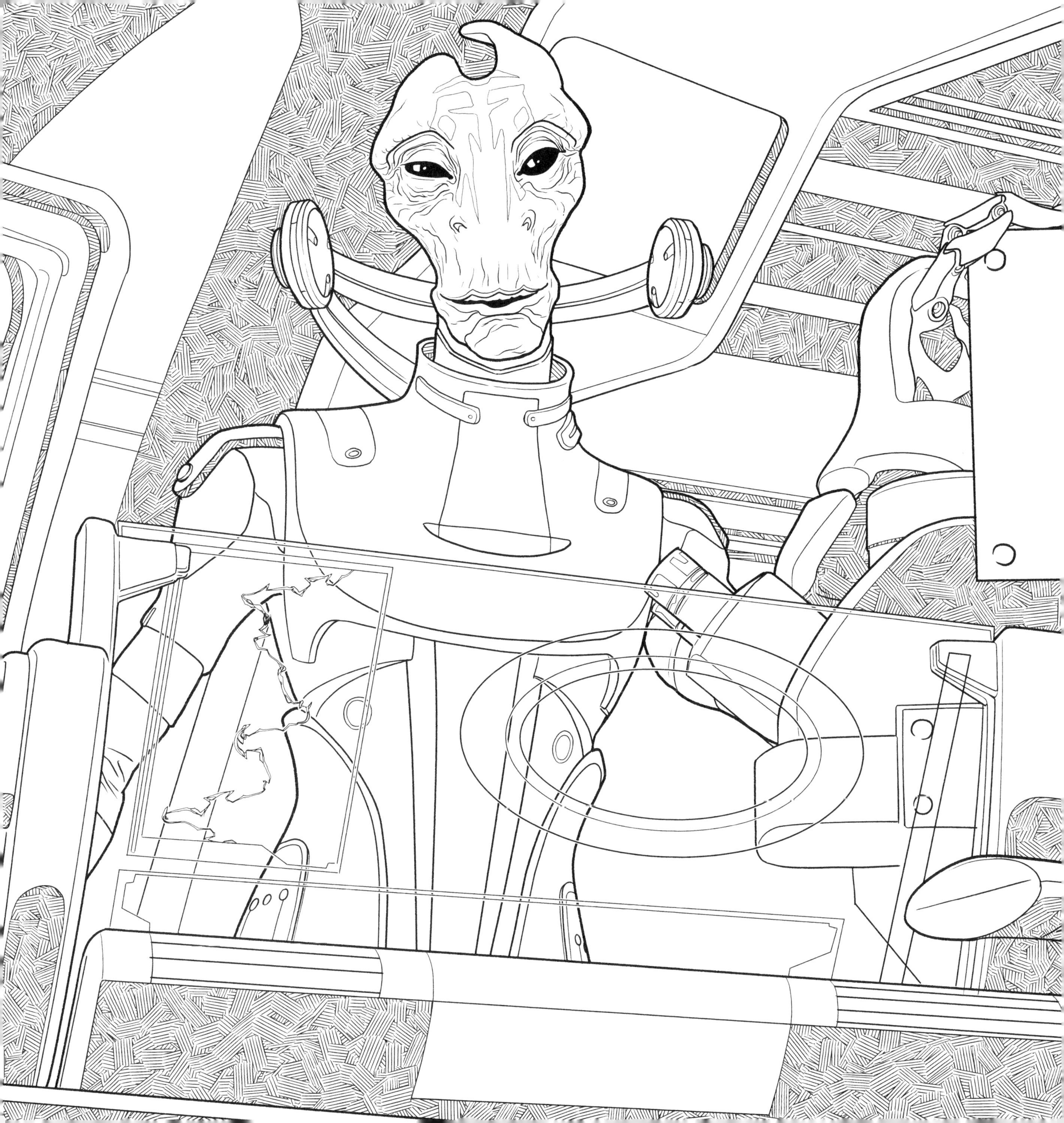

"Thank you, Shepard. You gave me purpose. Now let's find something big to kill."
—Grunt

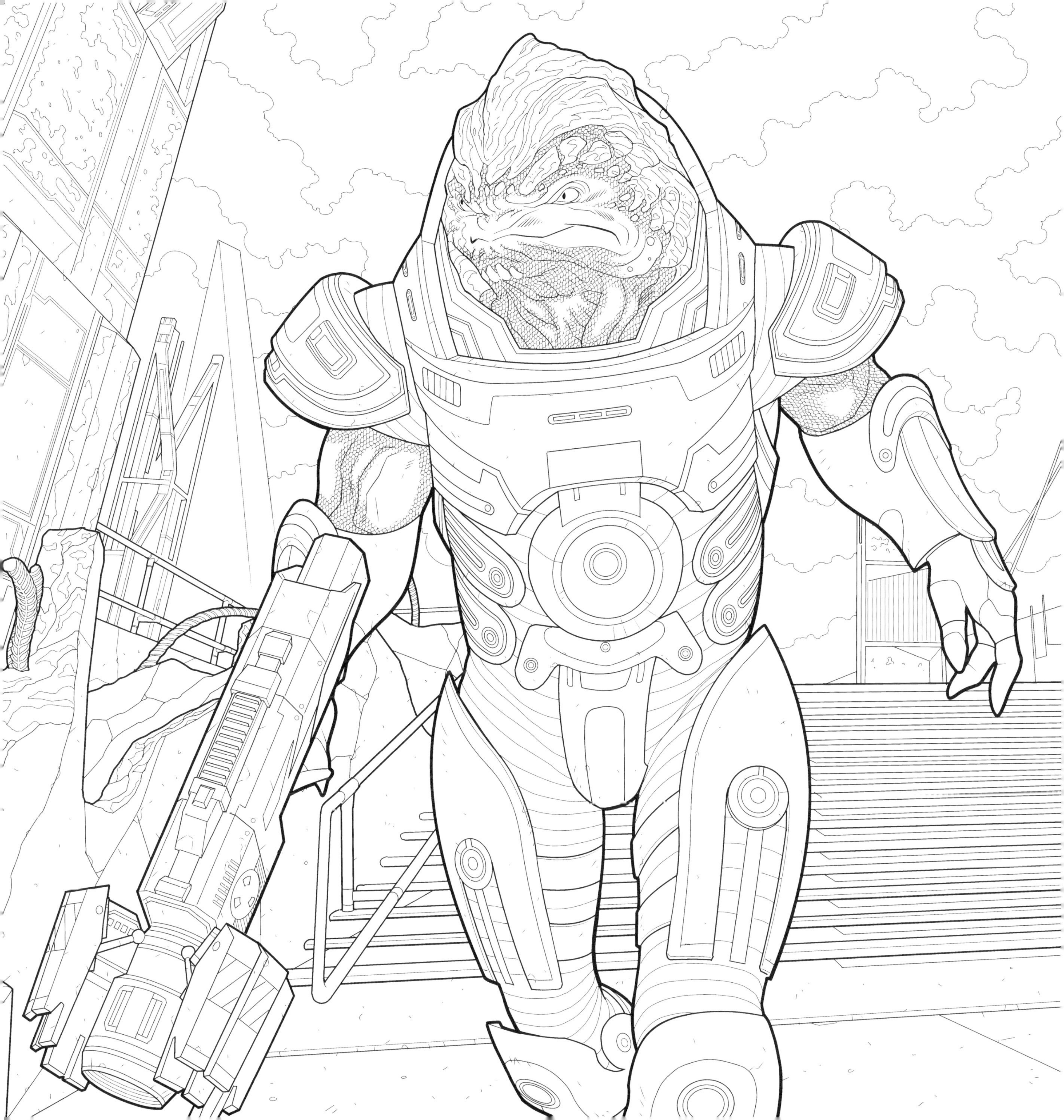

"I've been around. Ran around with gangs, wiped out some gangs, joined a cult. Kept the haircut."
—Jack

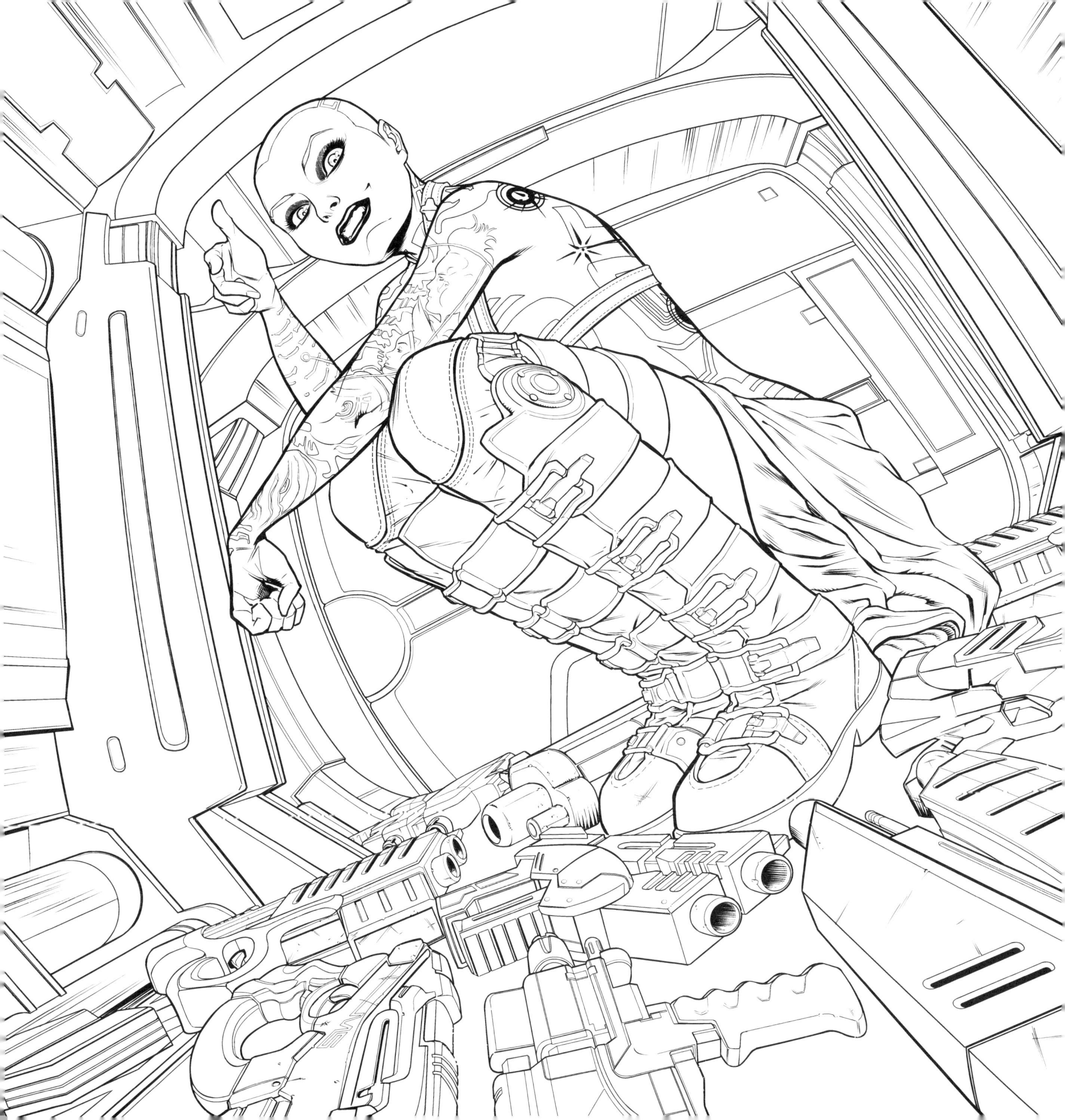

"By the code, I will serve you, Shepard. Your choices are my choices. Your morals are my morals. Your wishes are my code."
—Samara

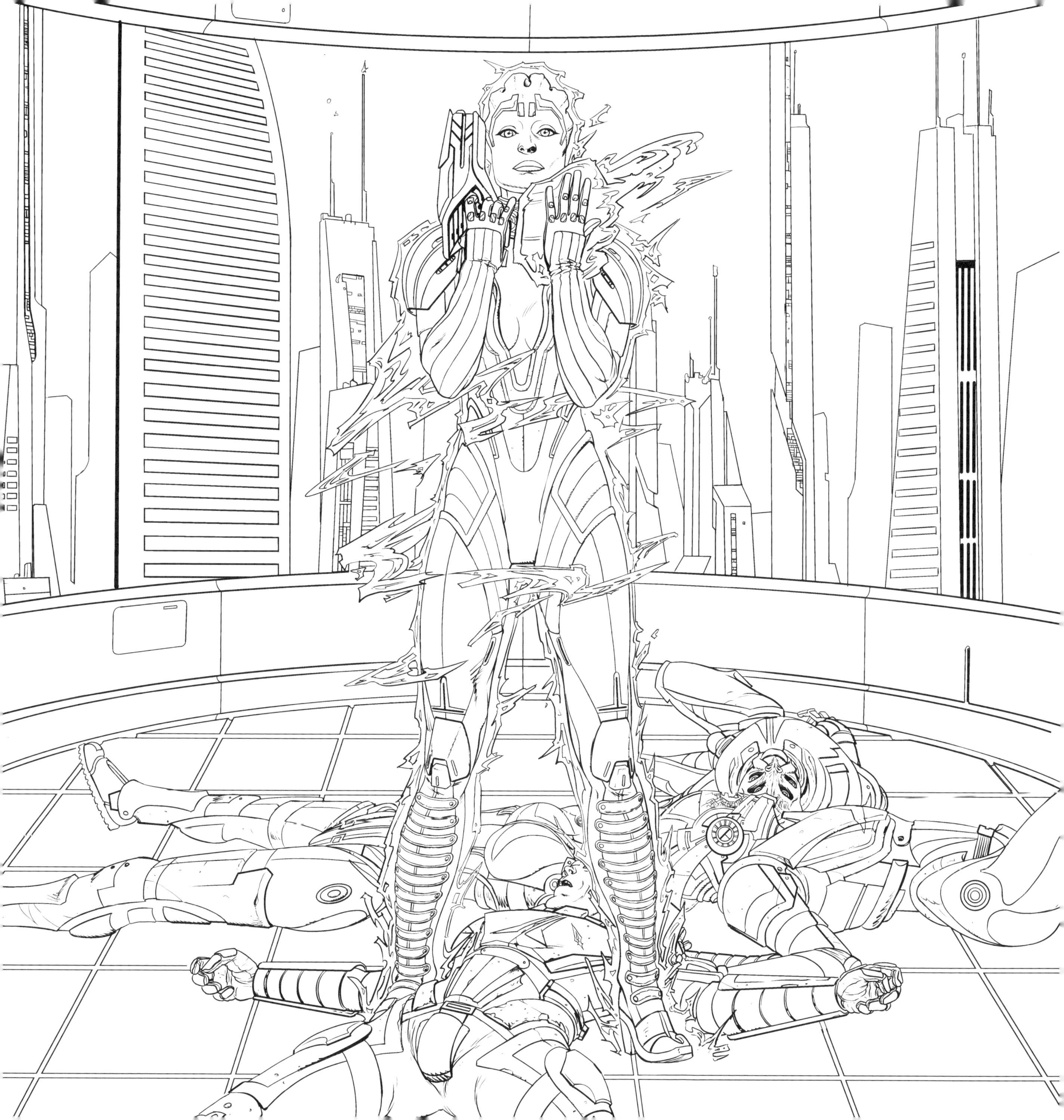

"The universe is a dark place. I'm trying to make it brighter before I die."
—Thane Krios

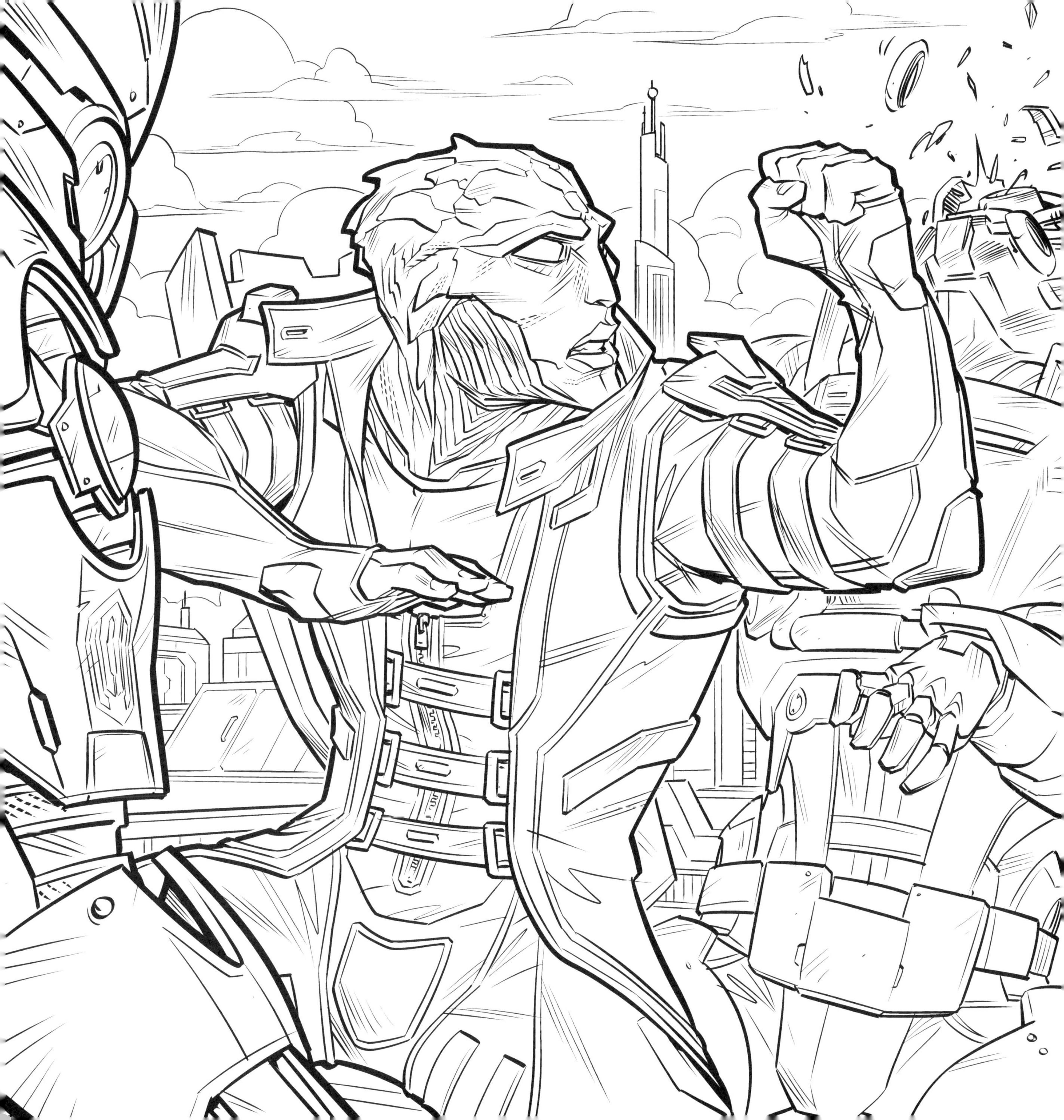

"We are Legion, a terminal of the geth. We will integrate into *Normandy*."

—Legion

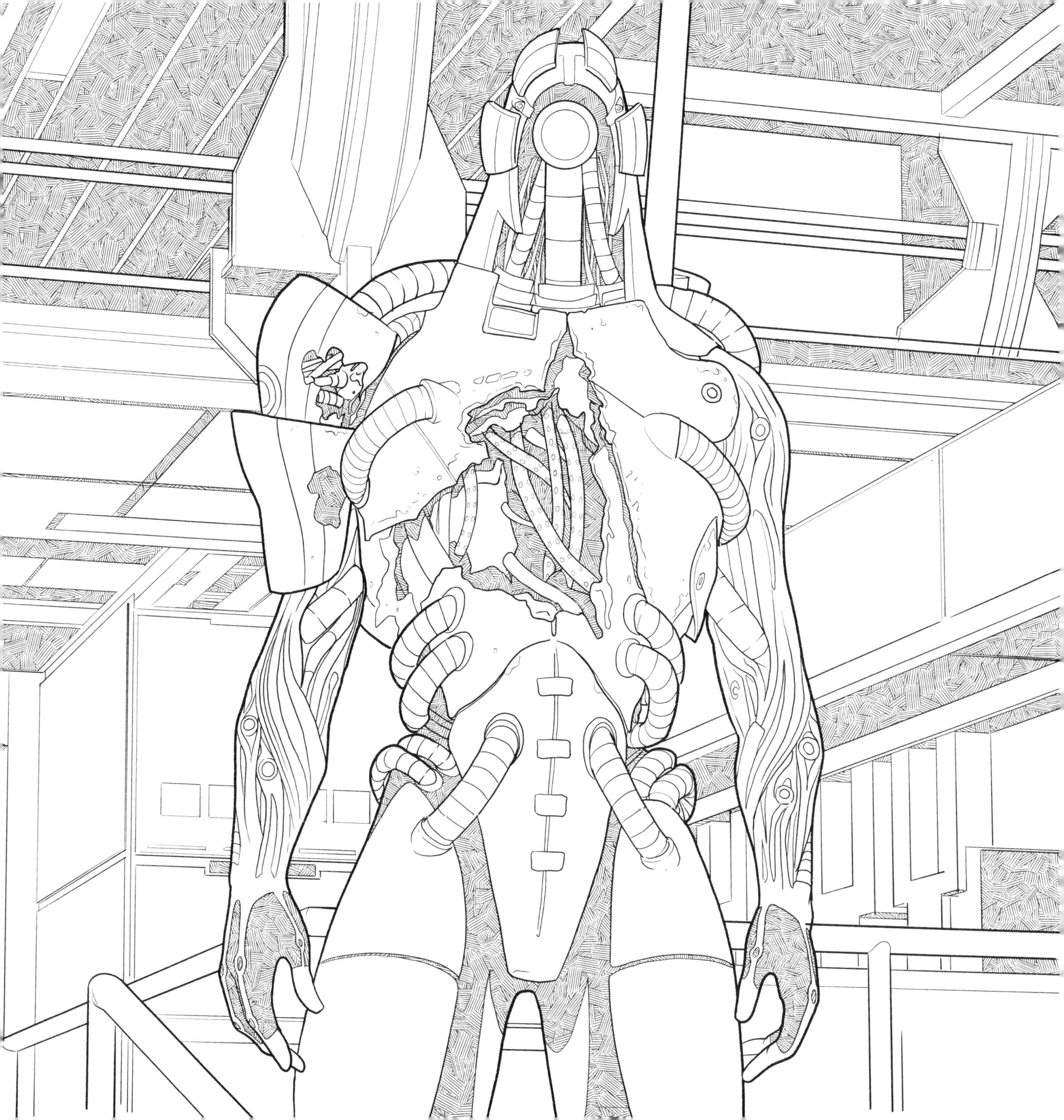

"A stubborn enough person will survive just about anythin'."
—Zaeed Massani

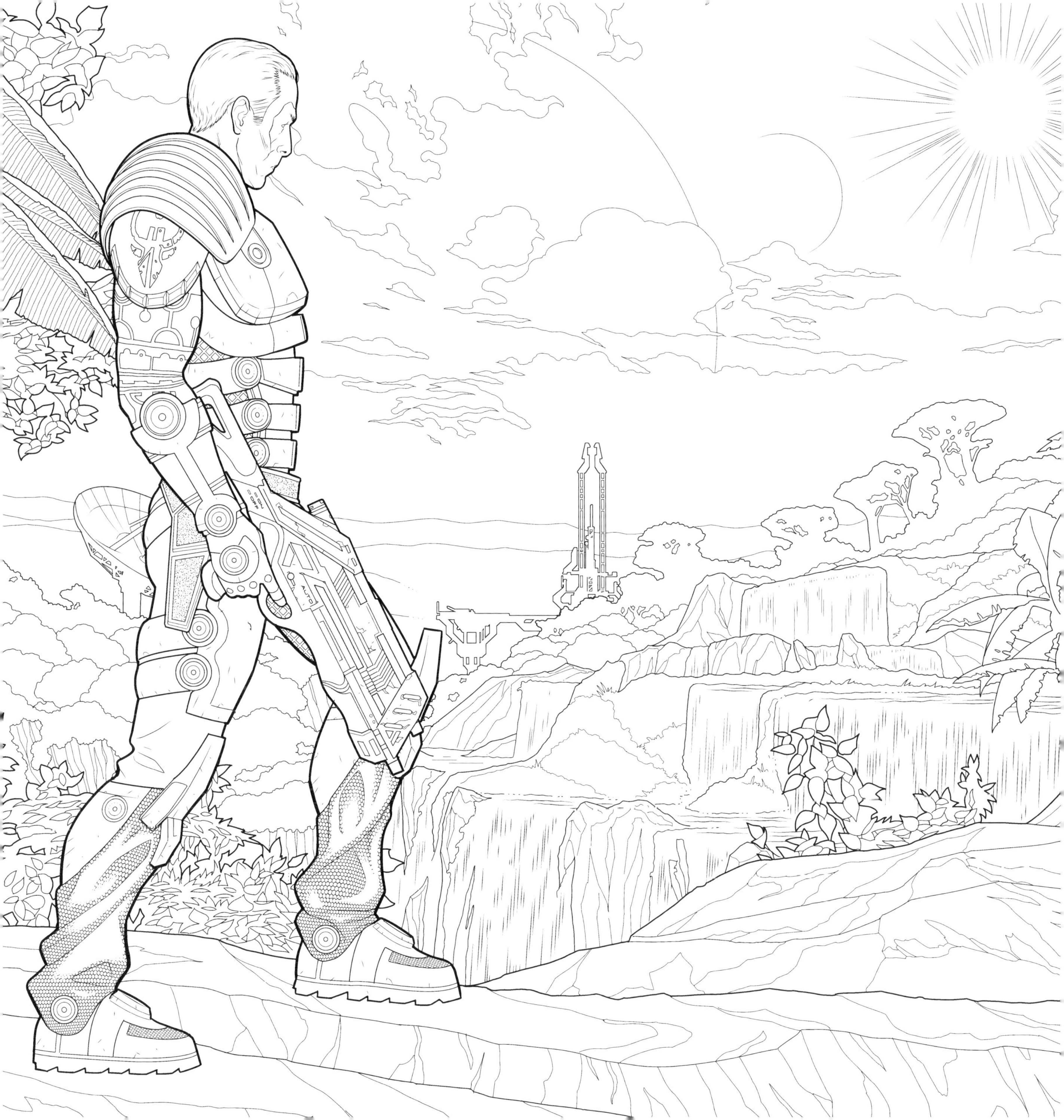
AUTO

"I'm the best thief in the business, not the most famous. Need to watch my step to keep it that way."
—Kasumi Goto

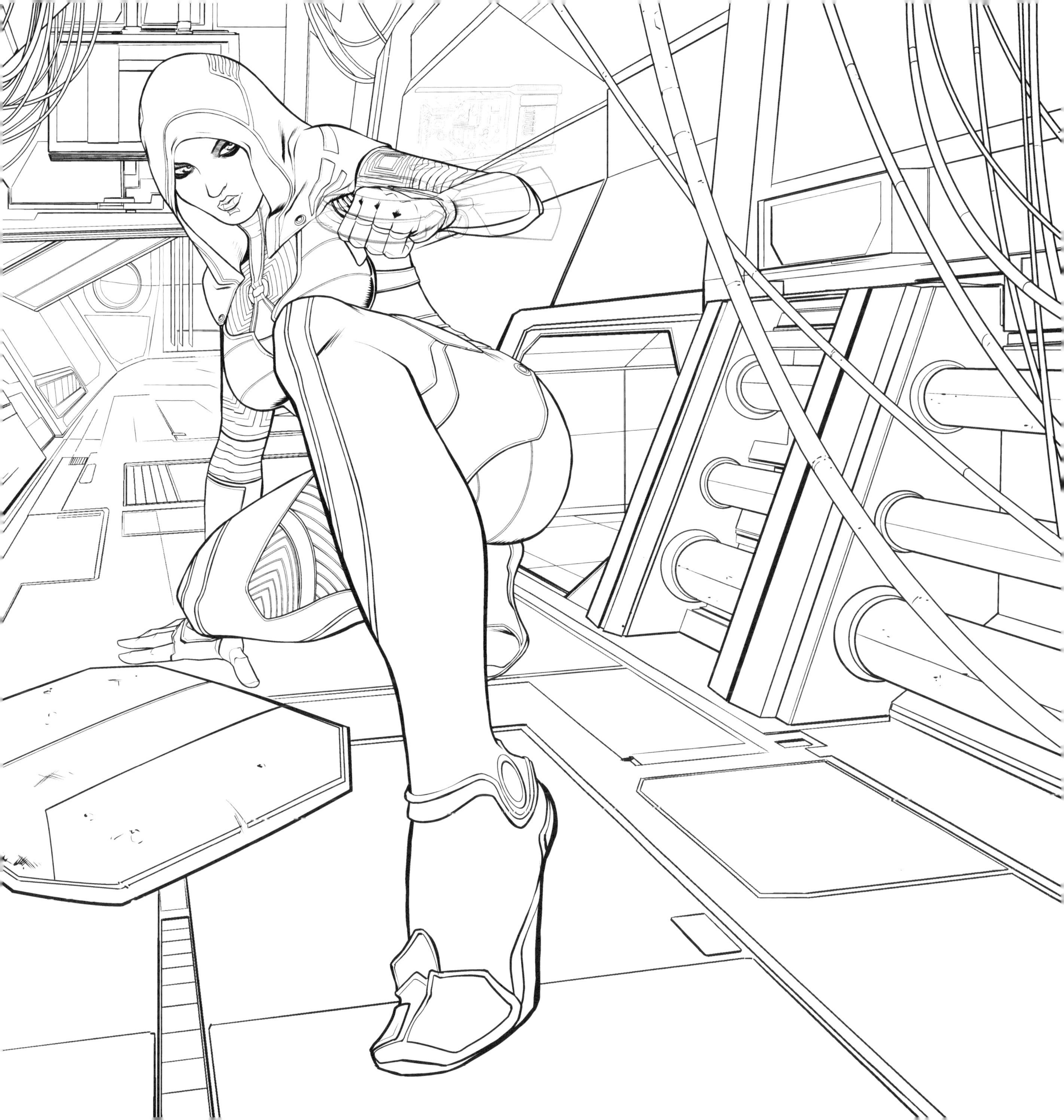

"Omega has no titled ruler and only one rule: Don't fuck with Aria!"

—Aria T'Loak

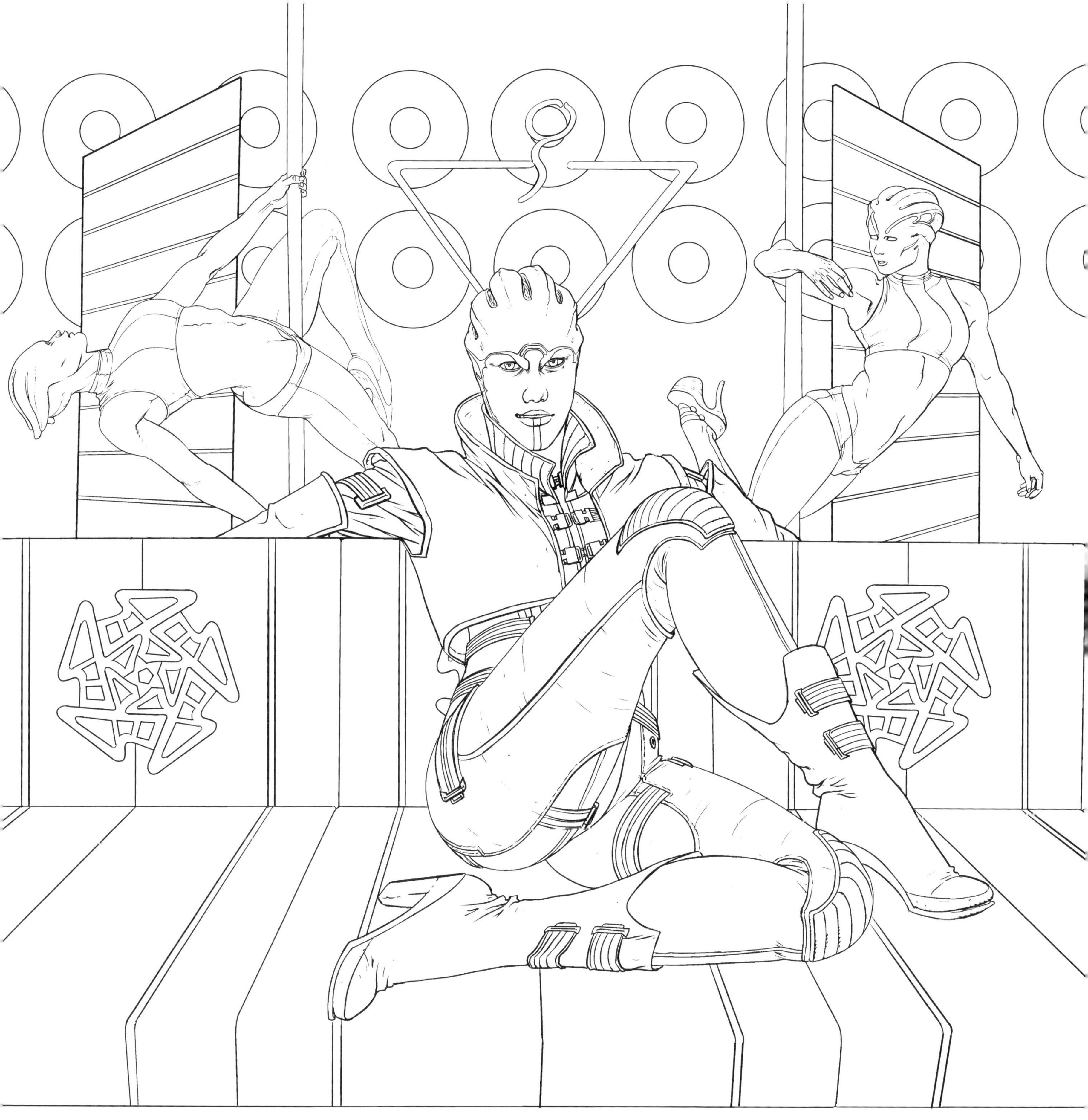

"That which you know as Reapers are your salvation through destruction."
—Harbinger

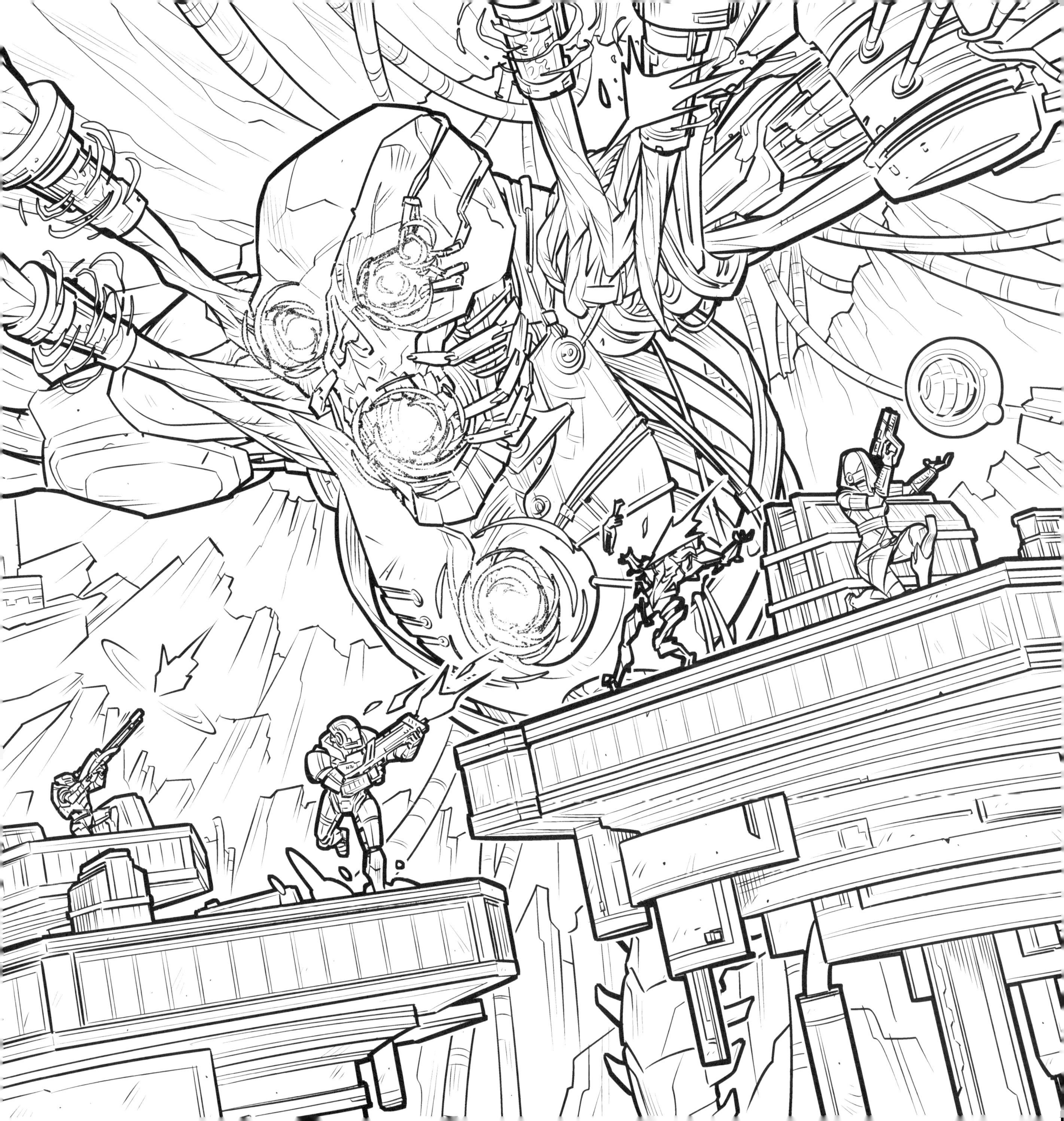

"You're kinda killing my mojo here, *jefe*."
—James Vega

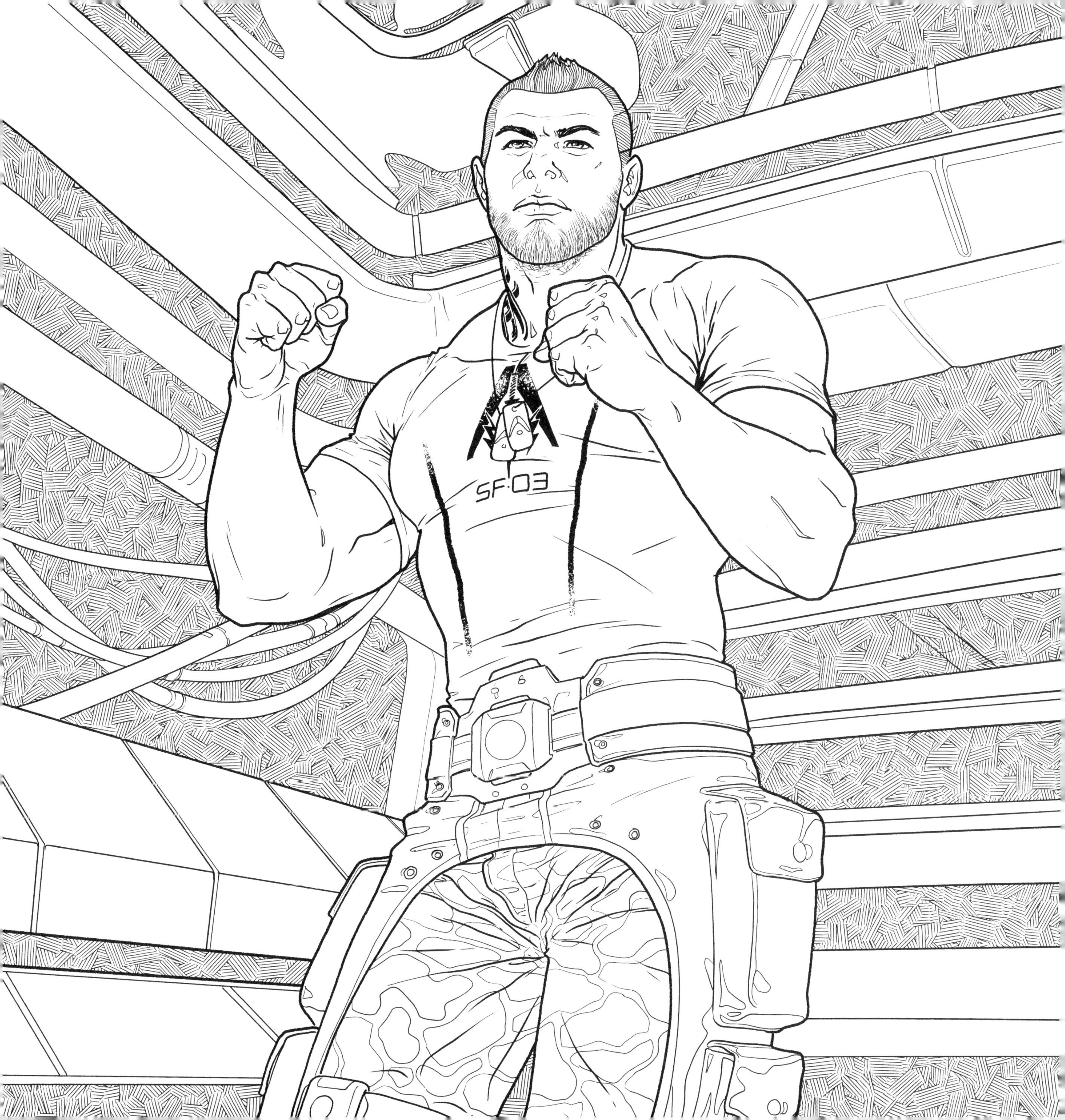
SF-03

"Stand in the ashes of a trillion dead souls and ask the ghosts if honor matters. The silence is your answer."

—Javik

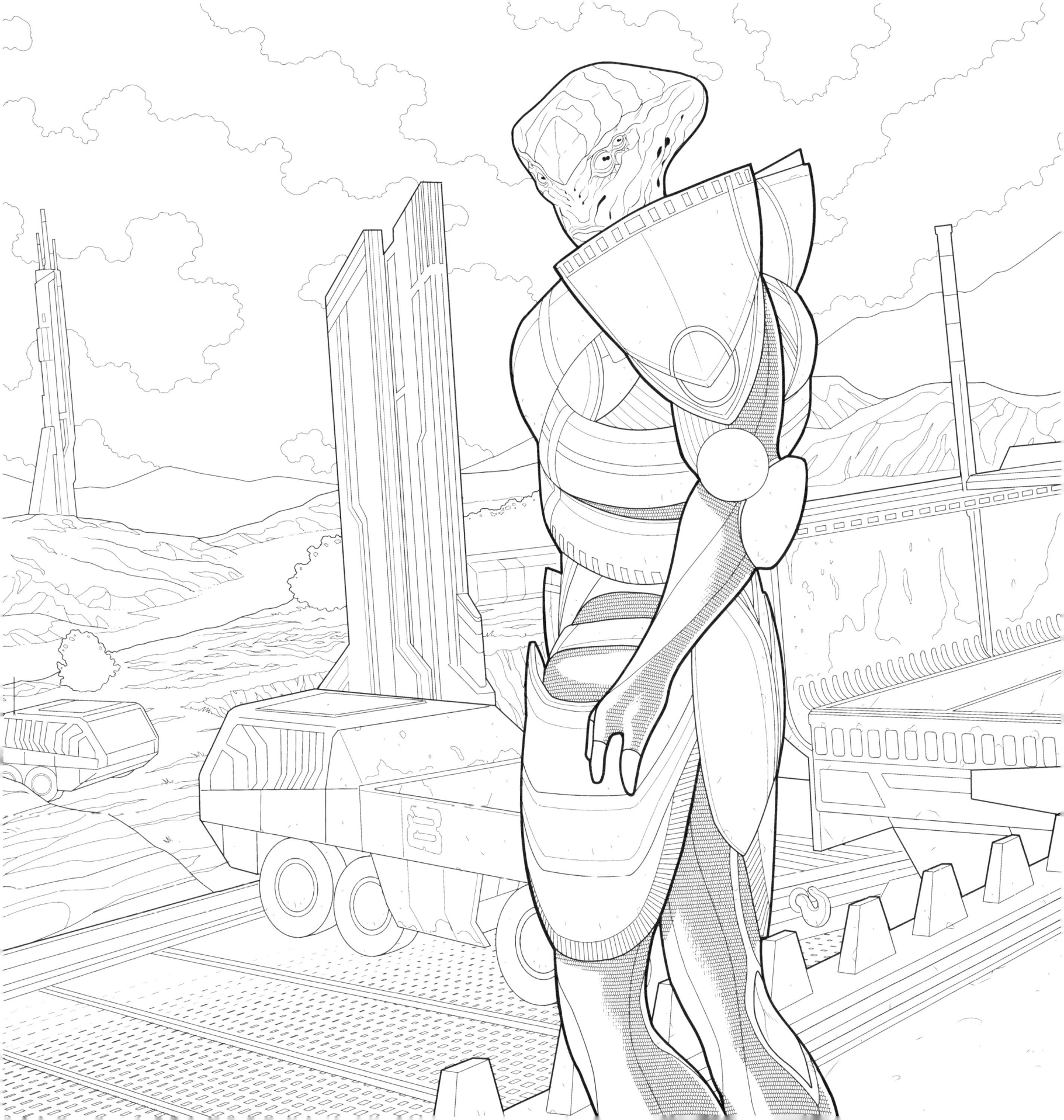

"Do not worry, Shepard. I only forget to recycle the *Normandy*'s oxygen when I've discovered something truly interesting. That was a joke."

—EDI

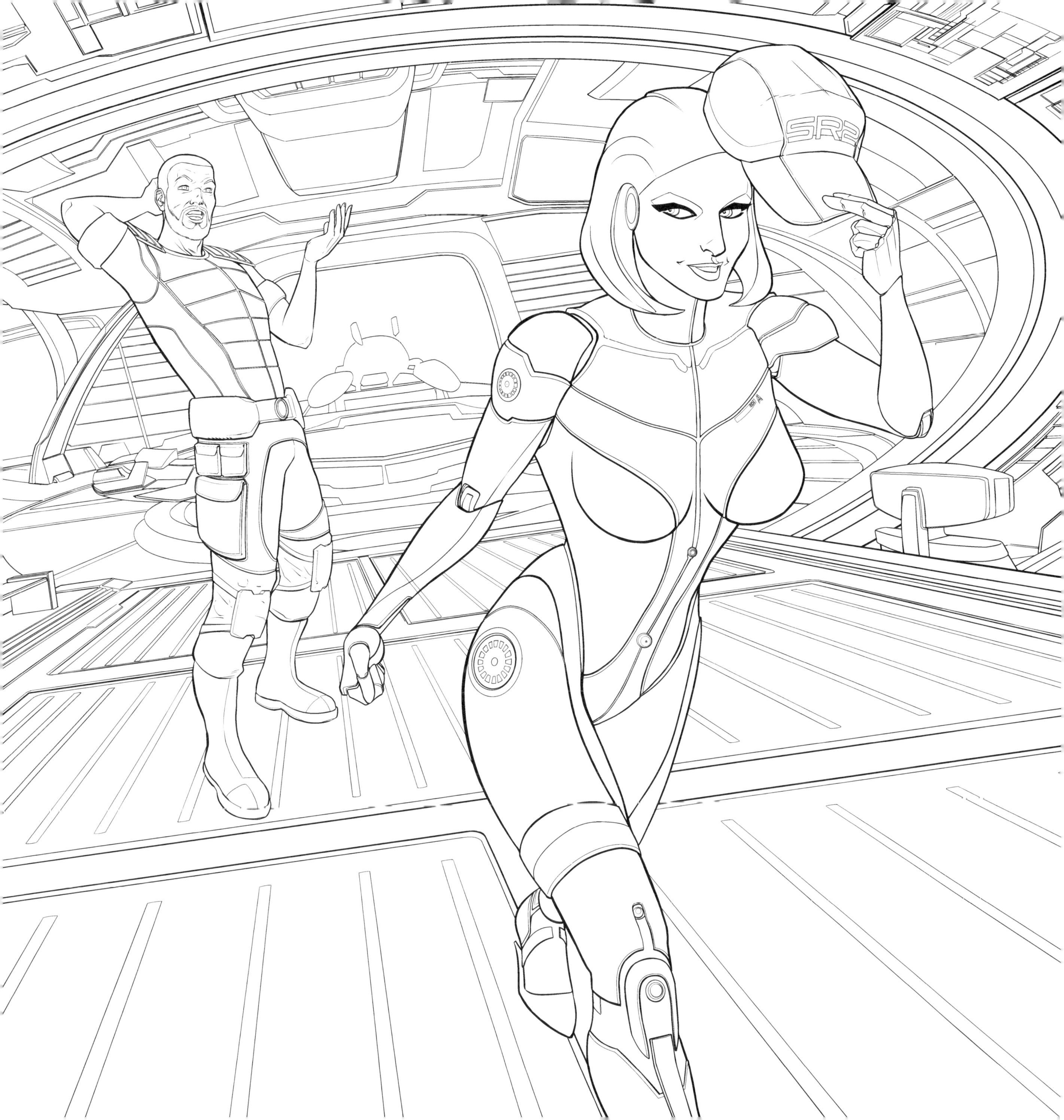
SR2

"I watched friends get turned into monsters—and I had to kill them. Now if you'll excuse me, I have an outpost to defend."

—Nyreen Kandros

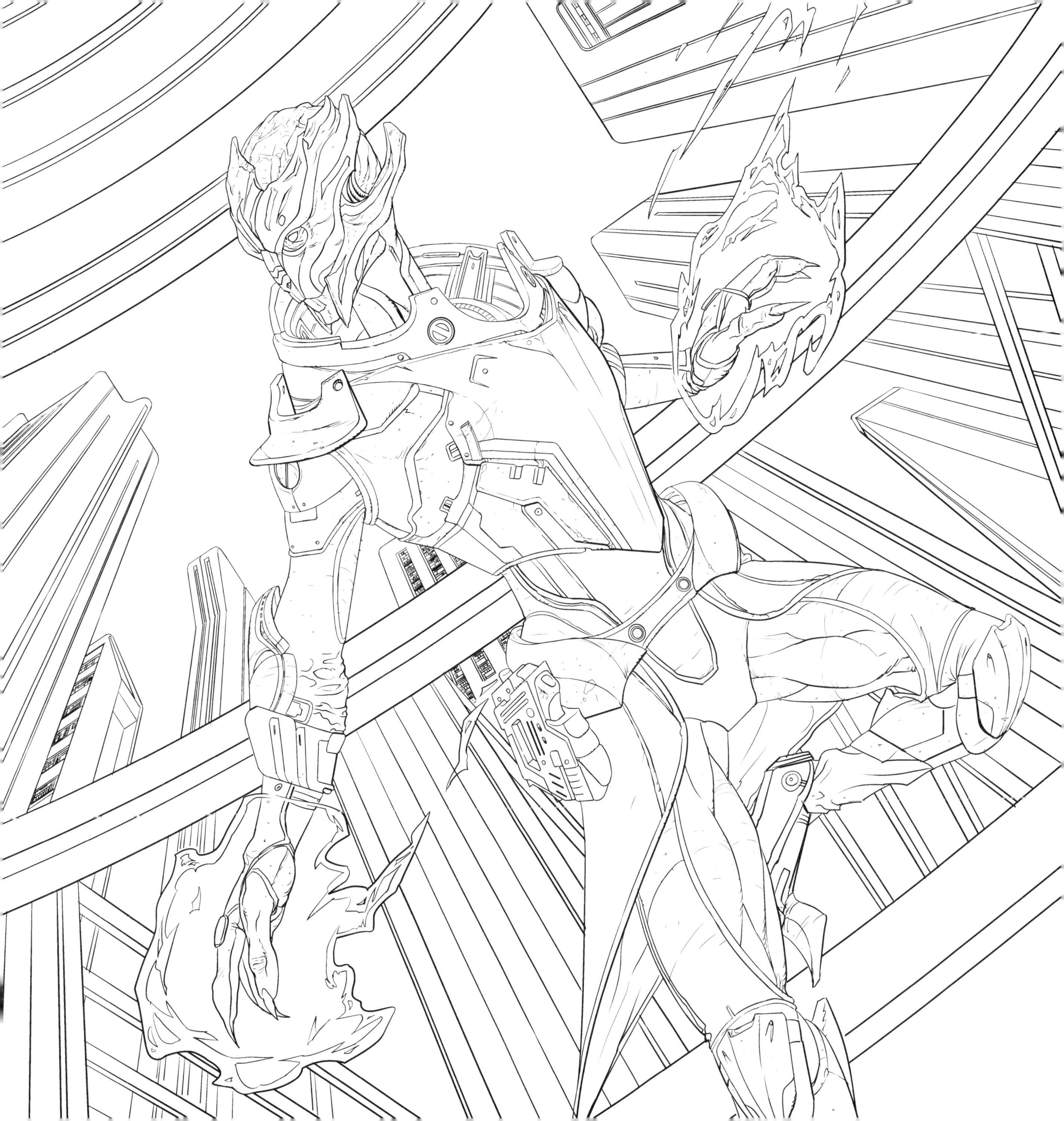

"I am Urdnot Wrex and this is my planet."
—Urdnot Wrex

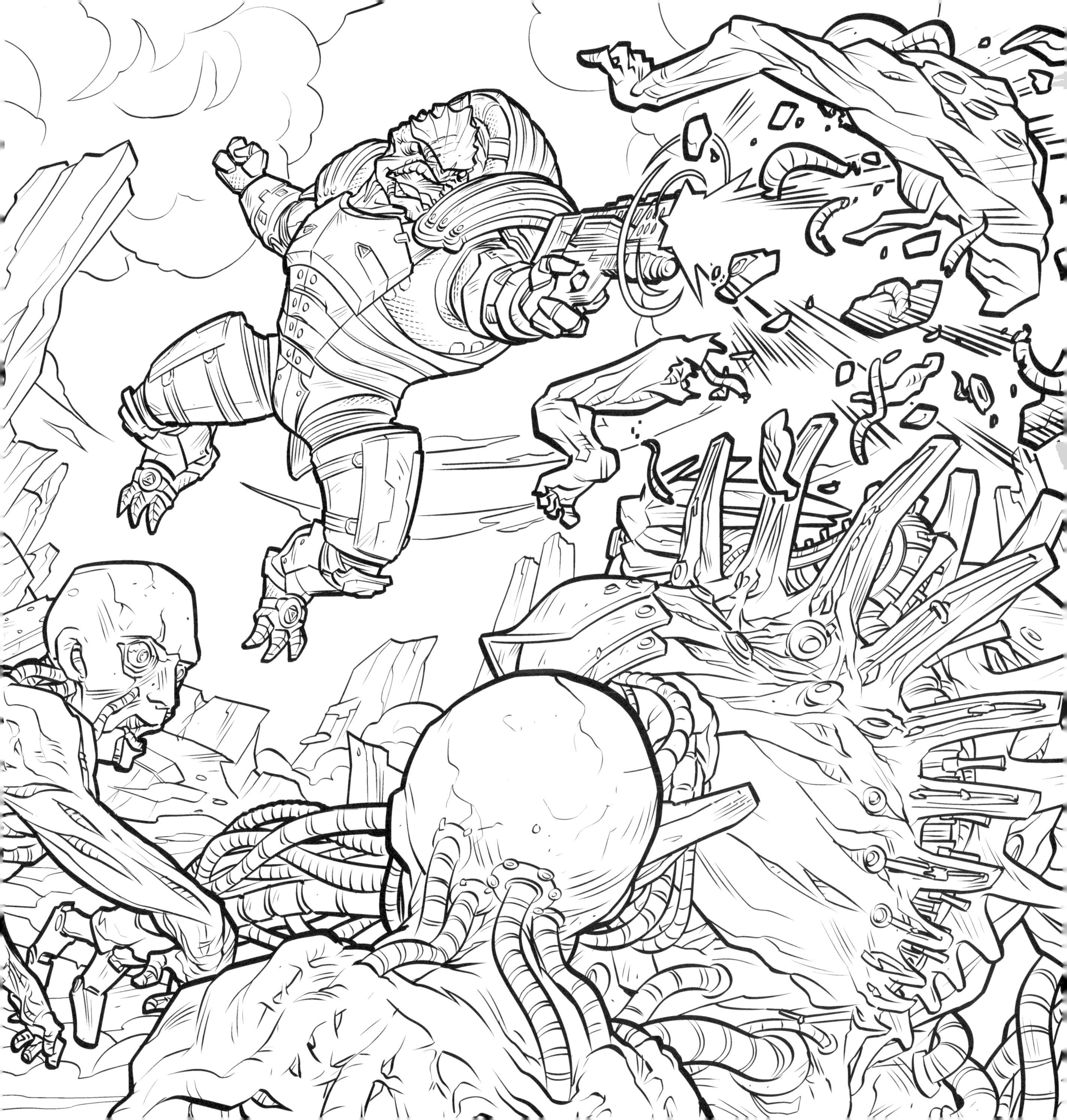

"What's on your mind, EDI?"
"The destruction of the Reaper on Tuchanka. It is rare for a technologically superior force to be destroyed by such an inferior one."
"Great, so now all we need is a gun that fires thresher maws."

—Commander Shepard, EDI, and Jeff "Joker" Moreau

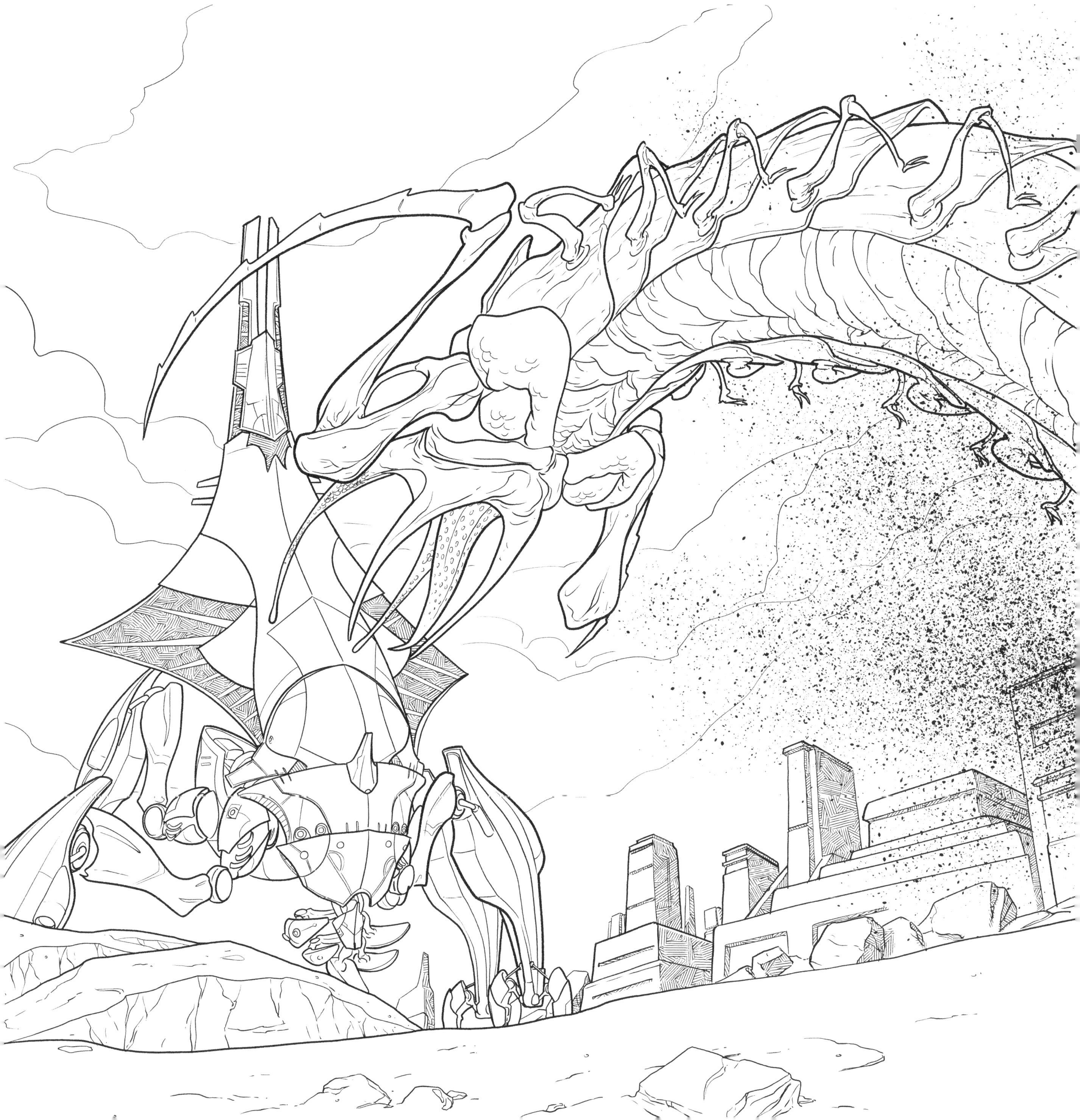

"Aware krogan females find scars attractive. Garrus loyal, reasonably intelligent. Bit aggressive. Almost like krogan."
"For the third time, Doctor, I'm not interested."
—Mordin Solus and Eve

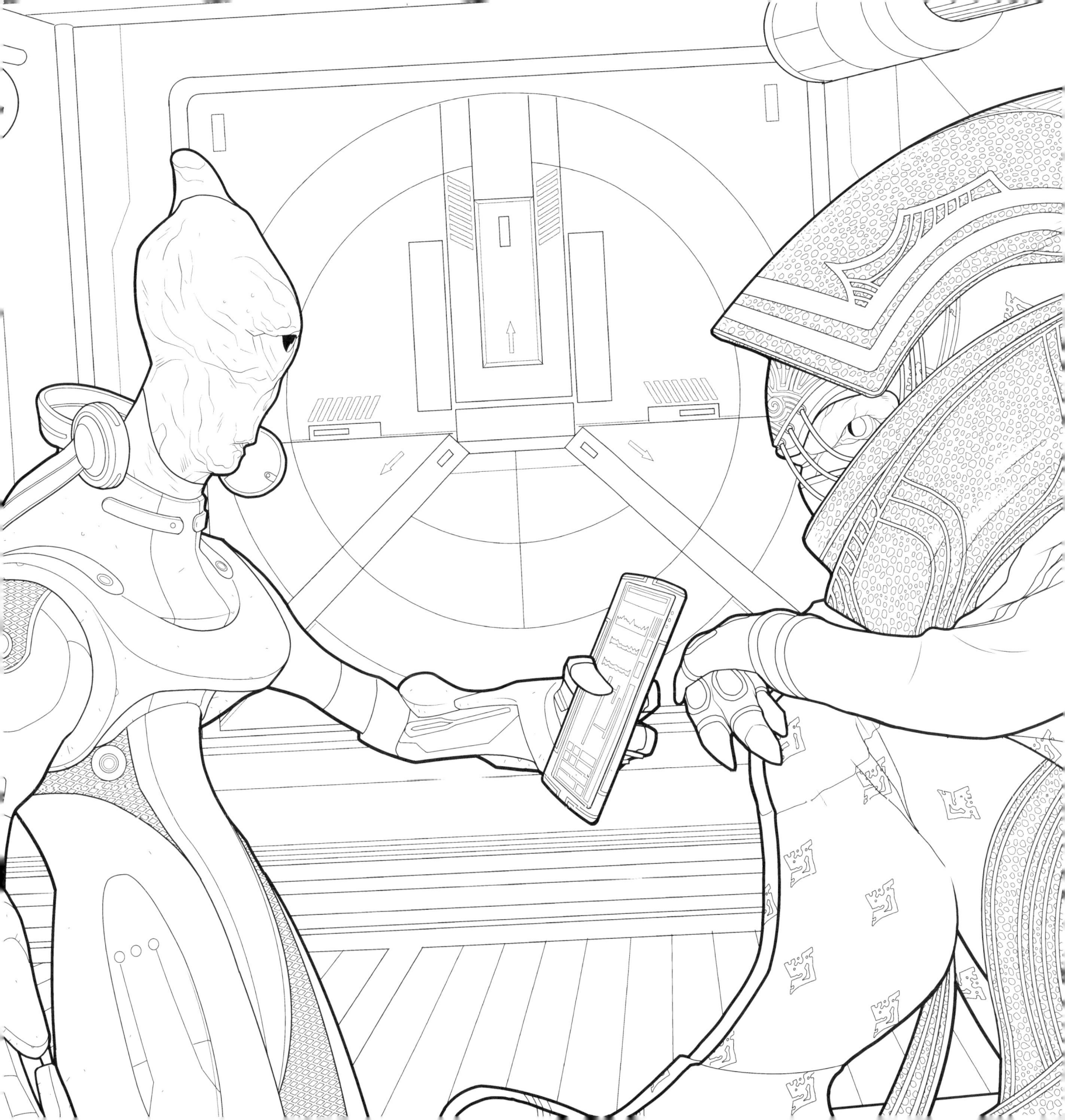

"You're slow, Shepard!"
—Kai Leng

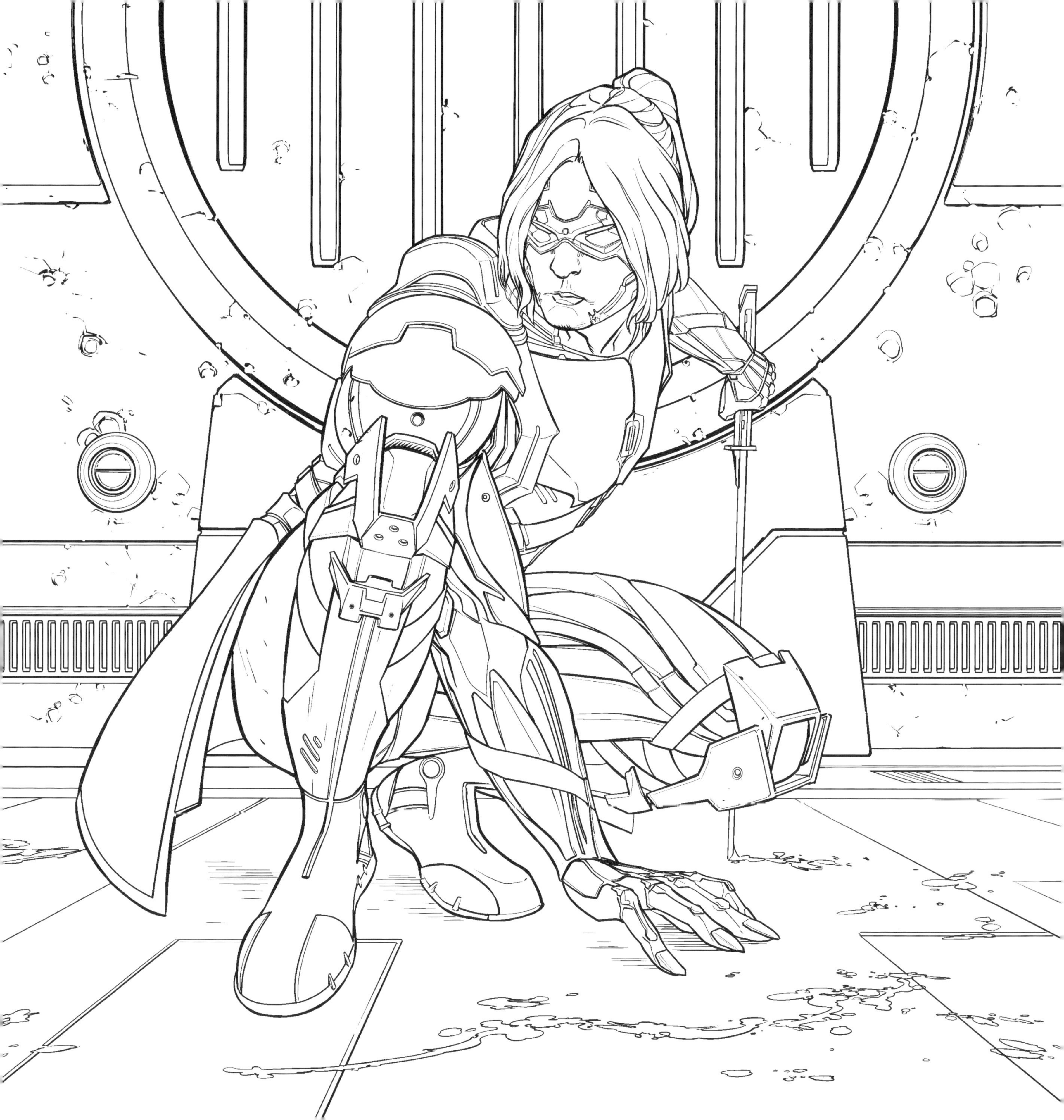

"We fight or we die! That's the plan!"
—Commander Shepard

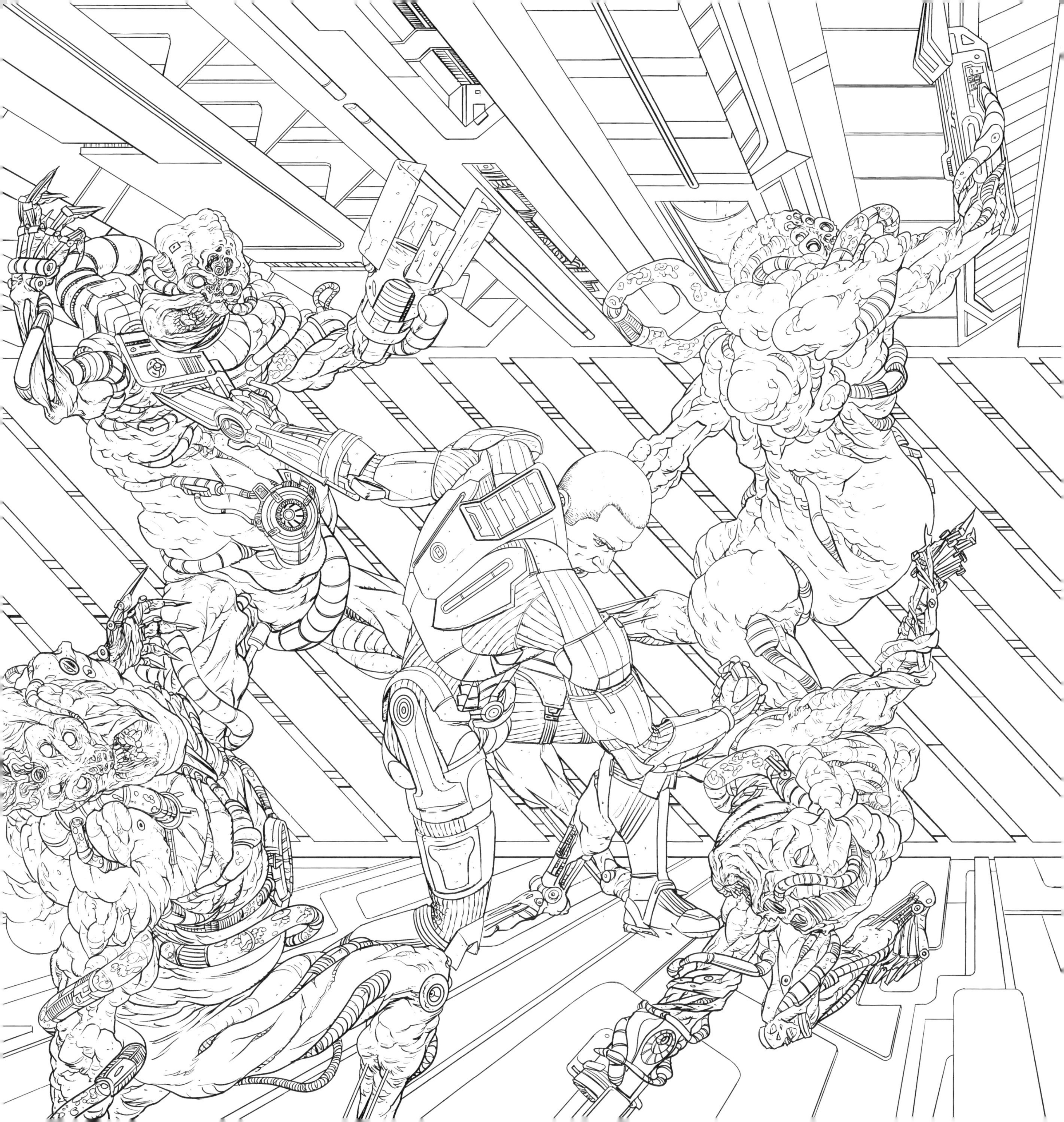

"Thanks for coming, everyone. Here's to us."
—Commander Shepard

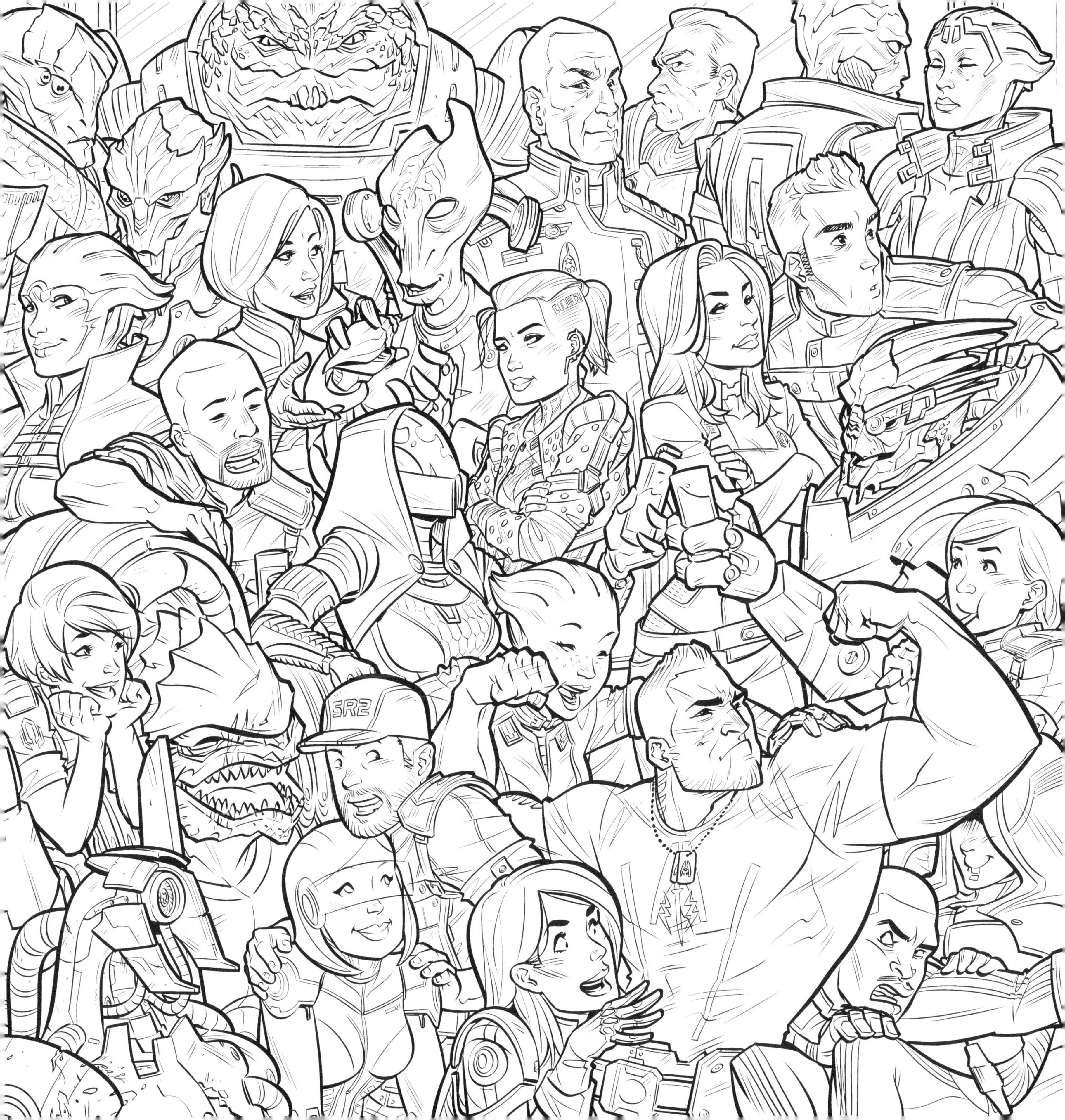
SR2

"We got here by reaching. We're explorers, not an army. That's not a weakness. It earned us everything."
—Scott Ryder

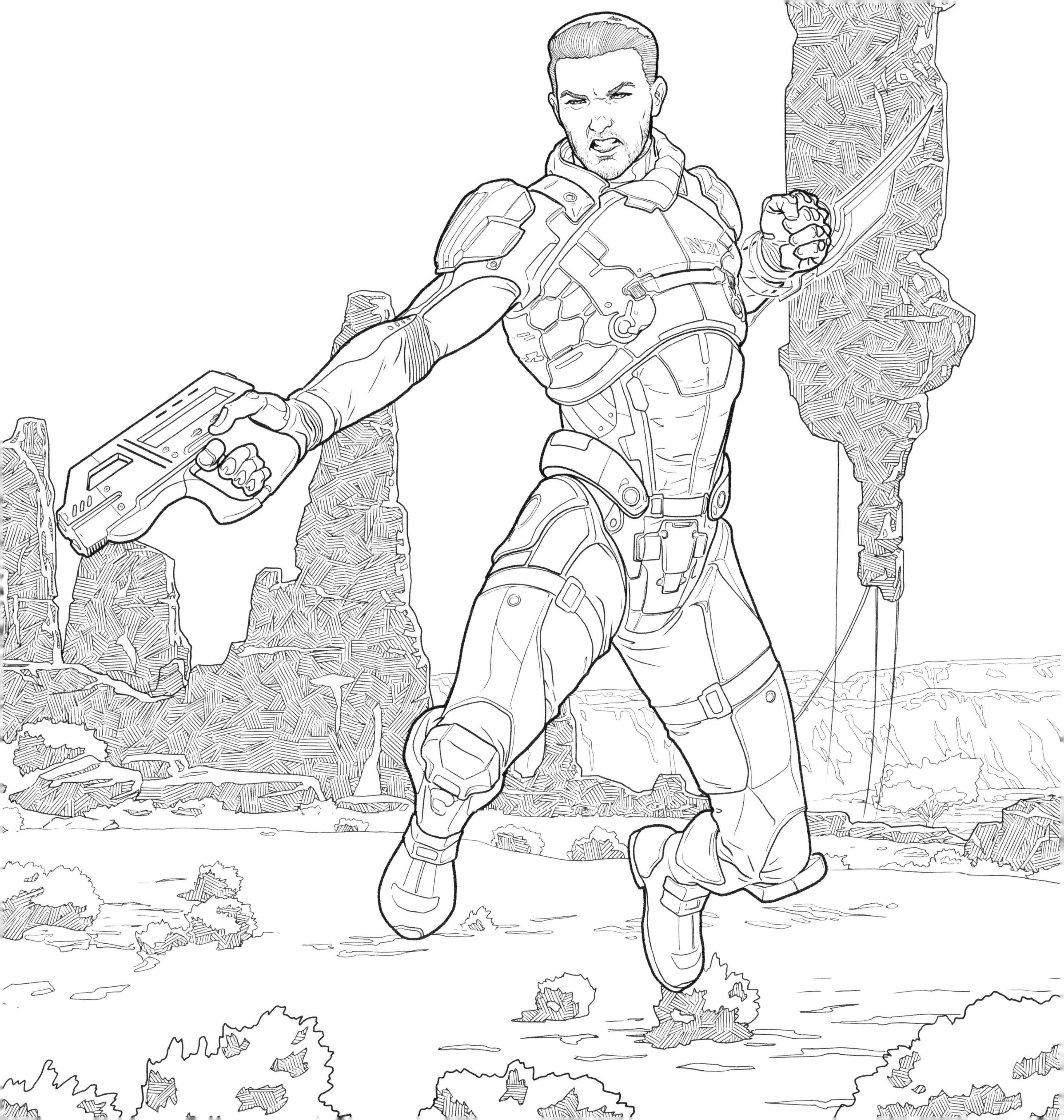

"We're fighting for the lives we've built. That only matters if there's someone left to live them."
—Sara Ryder

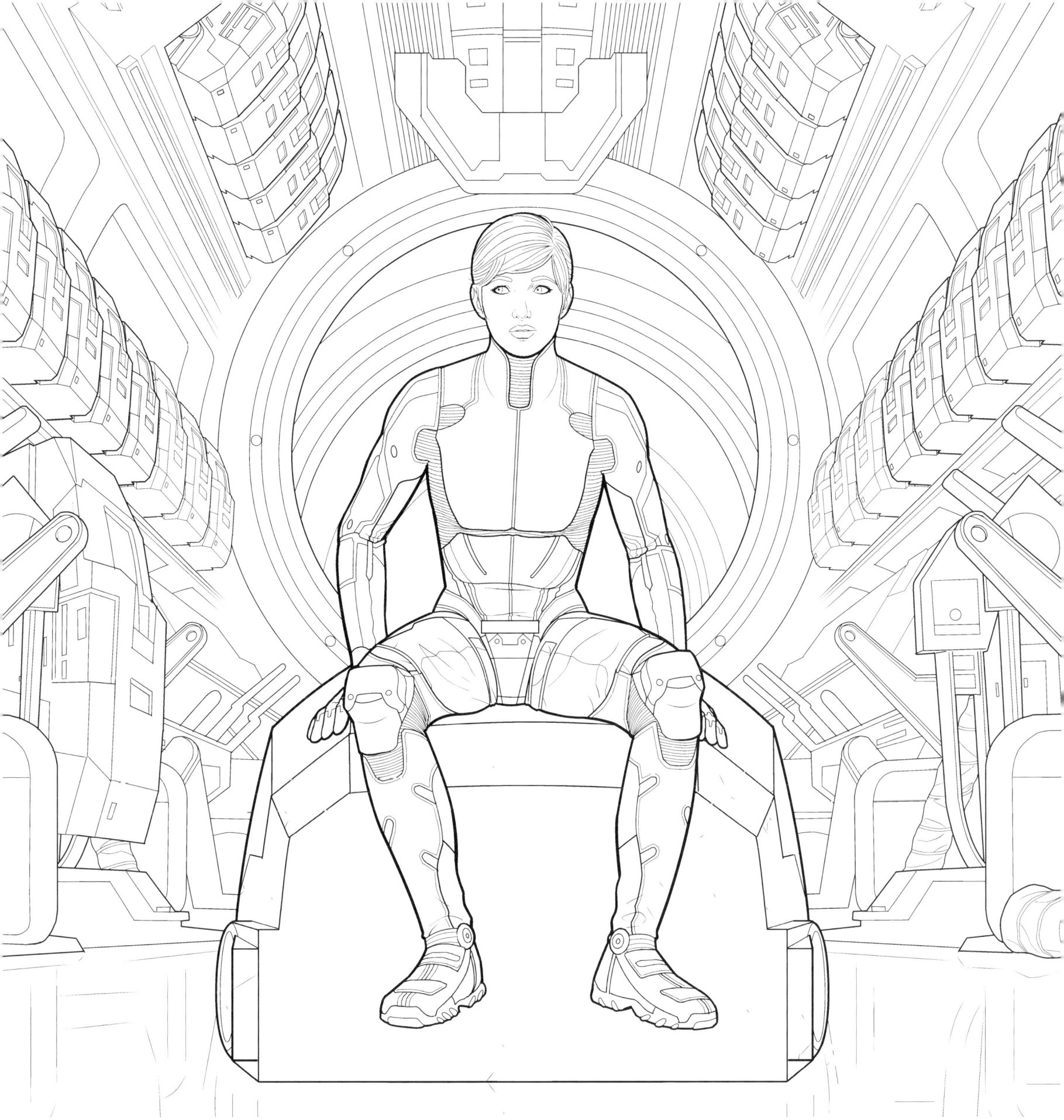

"I'm Jaal Ama Darav. I'll be your envoy through angaran space."
"Thank you for trusting me."
"I don't. But I can always kill you in your sleep."
"Good to know."
—Jaal and Ryder

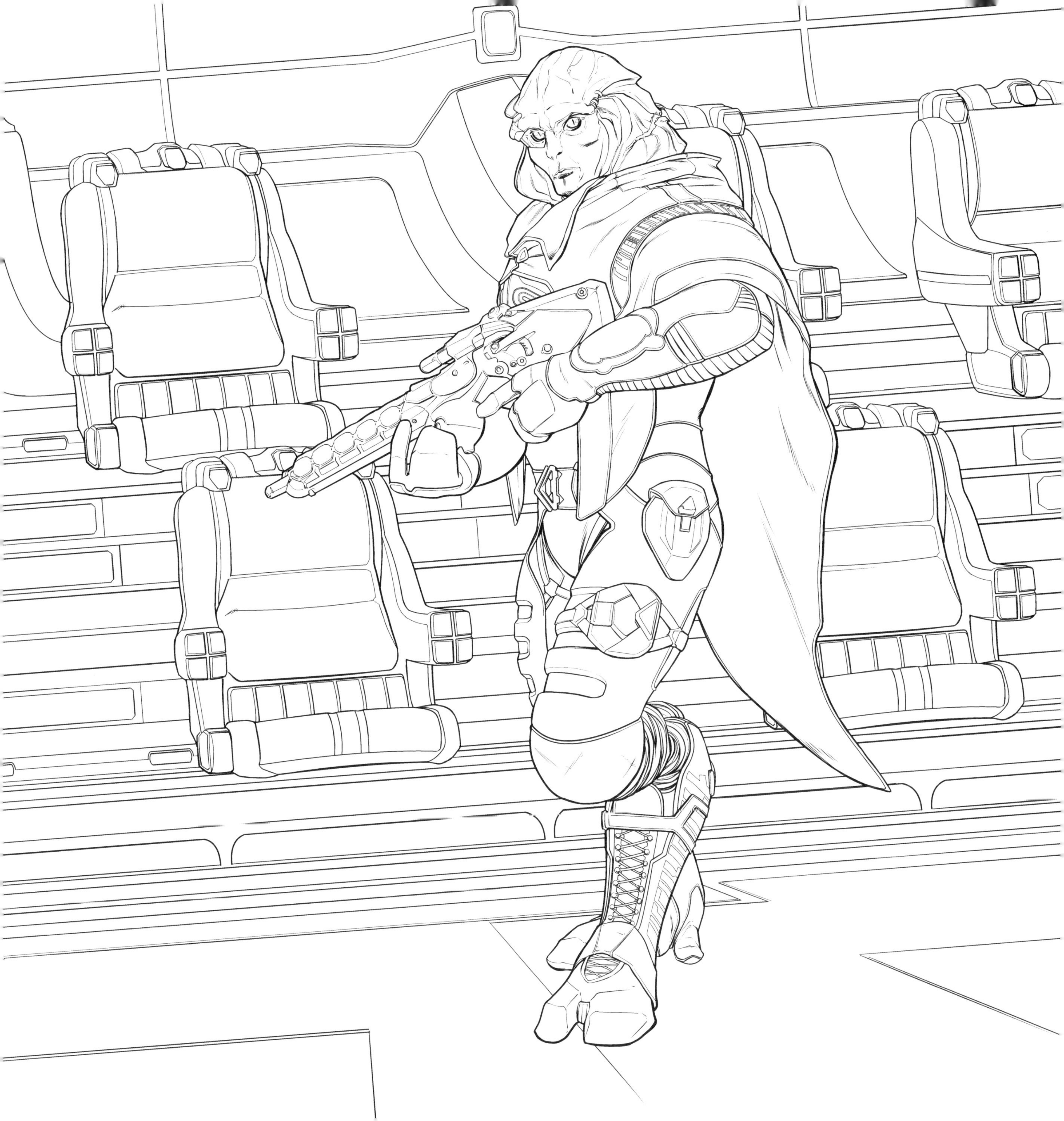

"Back off—it's mine."
  —Pelessaria B'Sayle

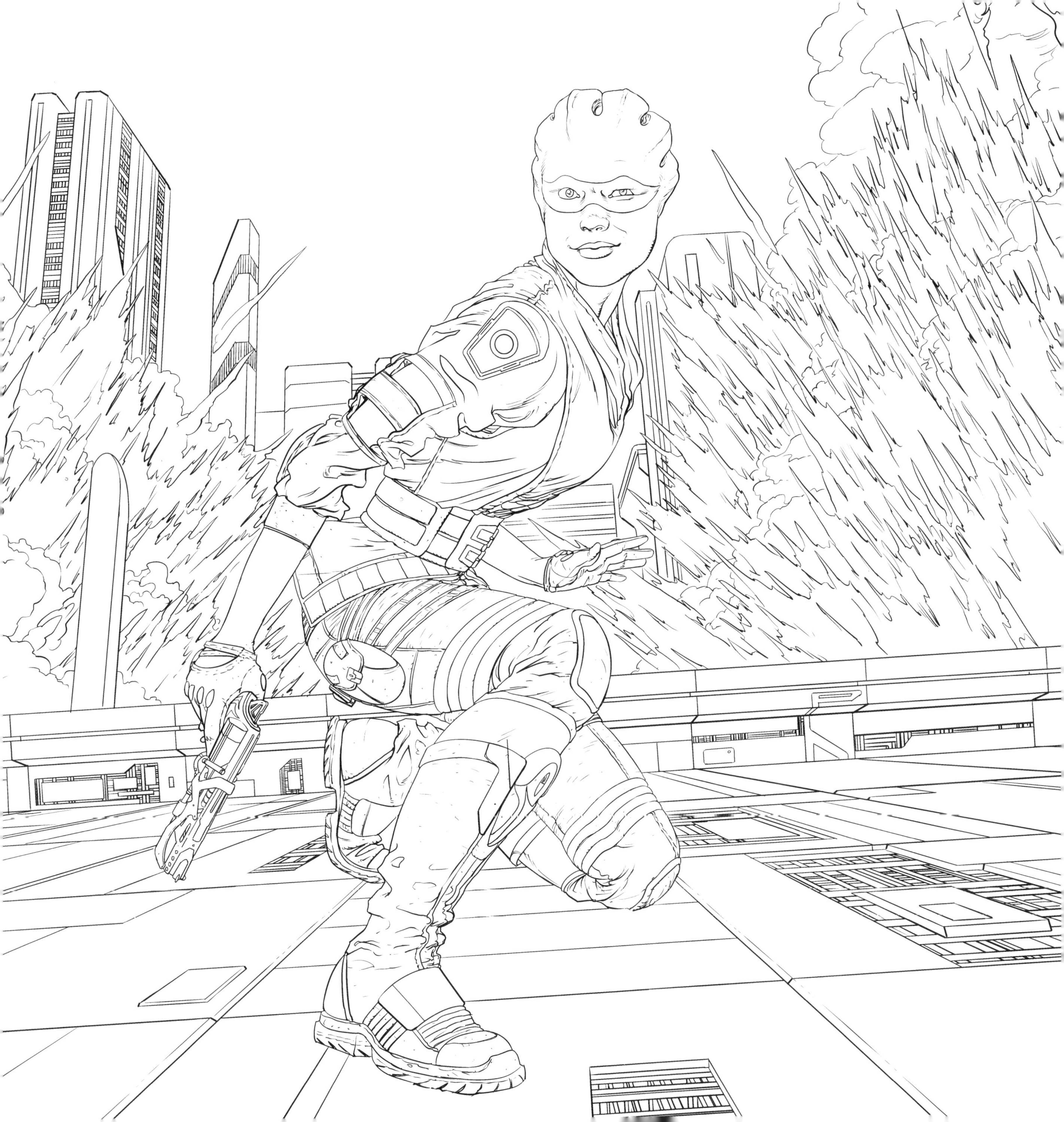

"I wasn't looking to start over. I wanted to start big."
—Liam

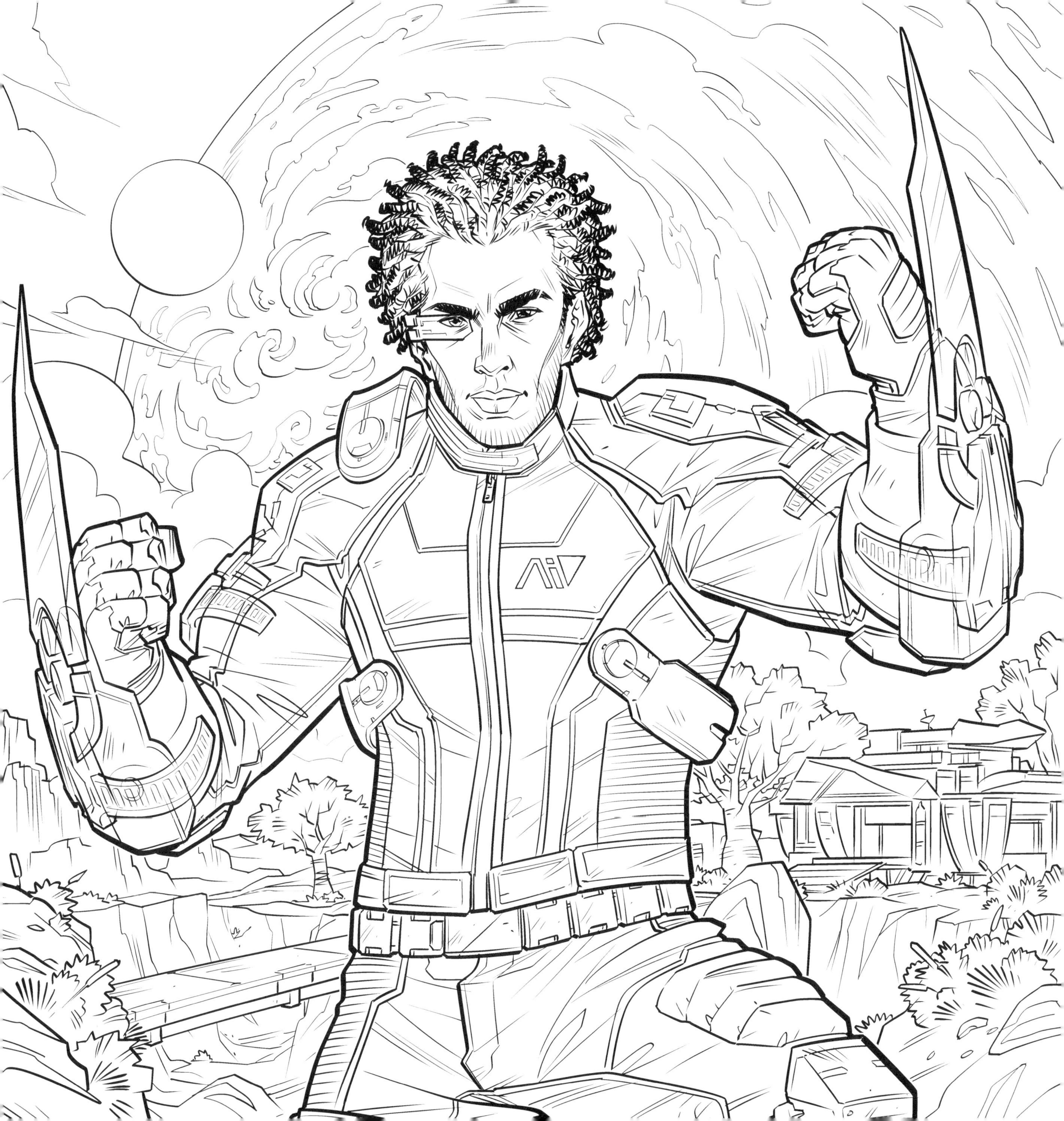

"I may be old, but my plating's still plenty hard."
—Drack

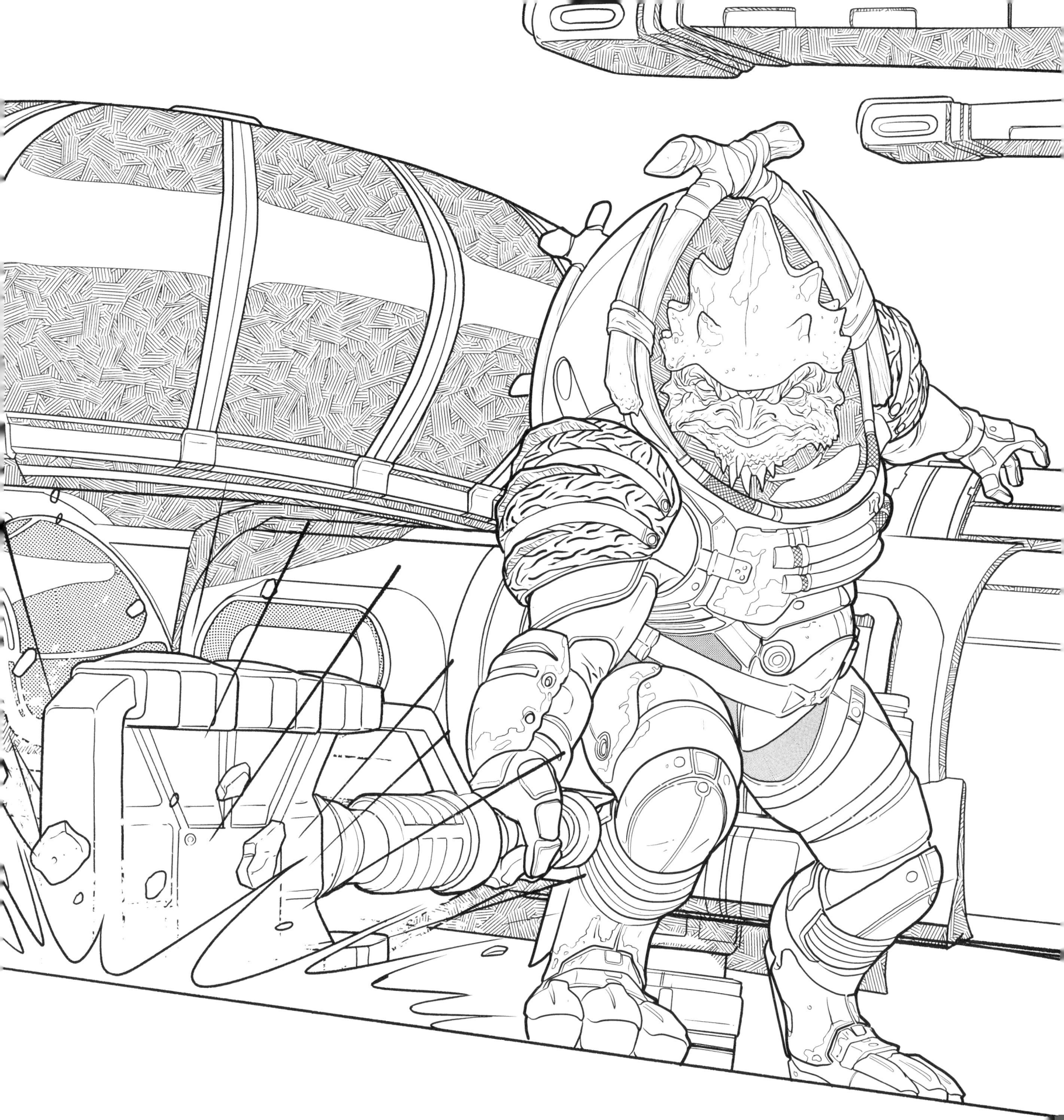

"I'm Vetra Nyx. Initiative wrangler, provisioner, gunner, and everything in between."
—Vetra Nyx

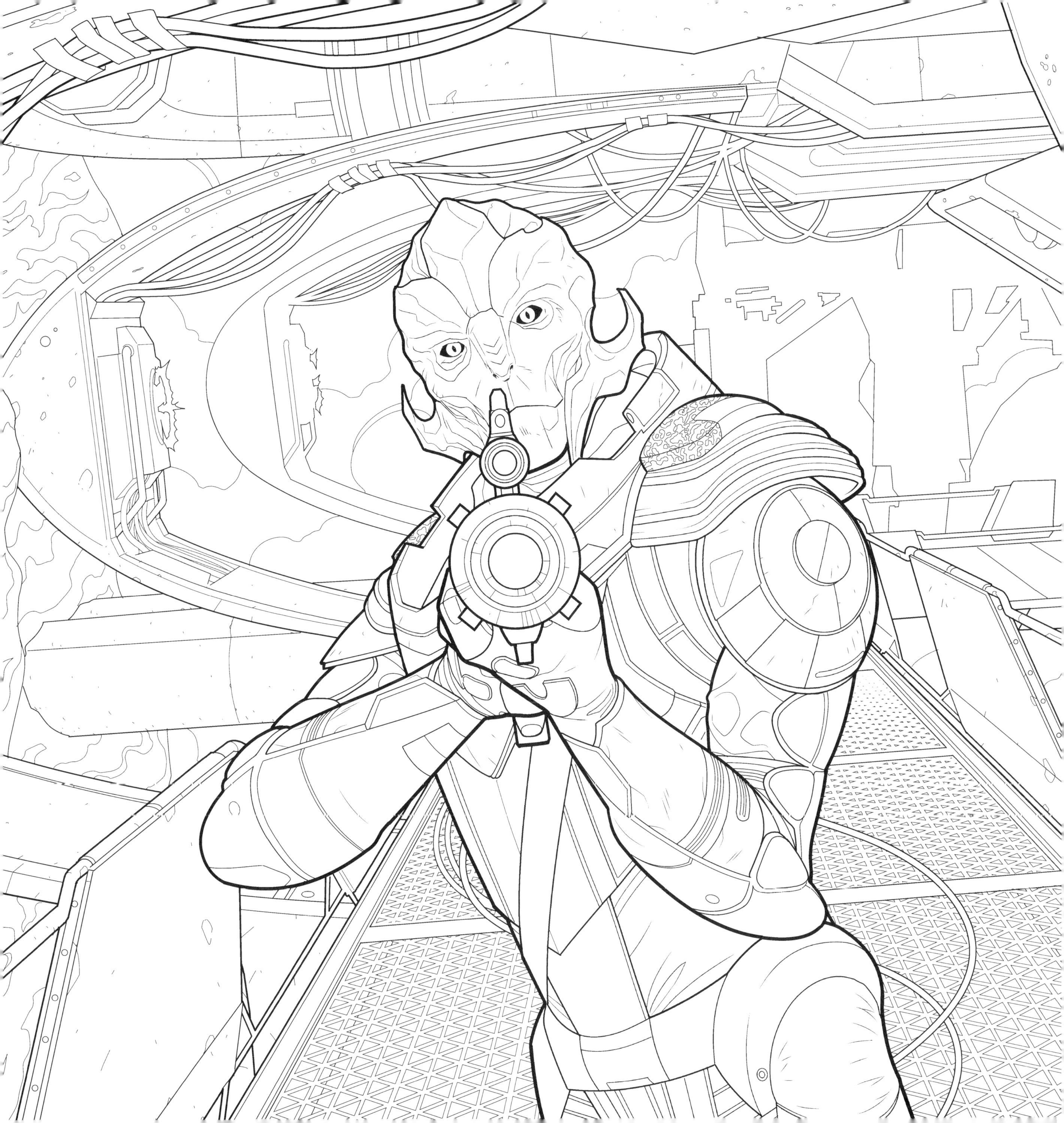

"We'll show them how it's done, Pathfinder. Always do."
—Cora Harper

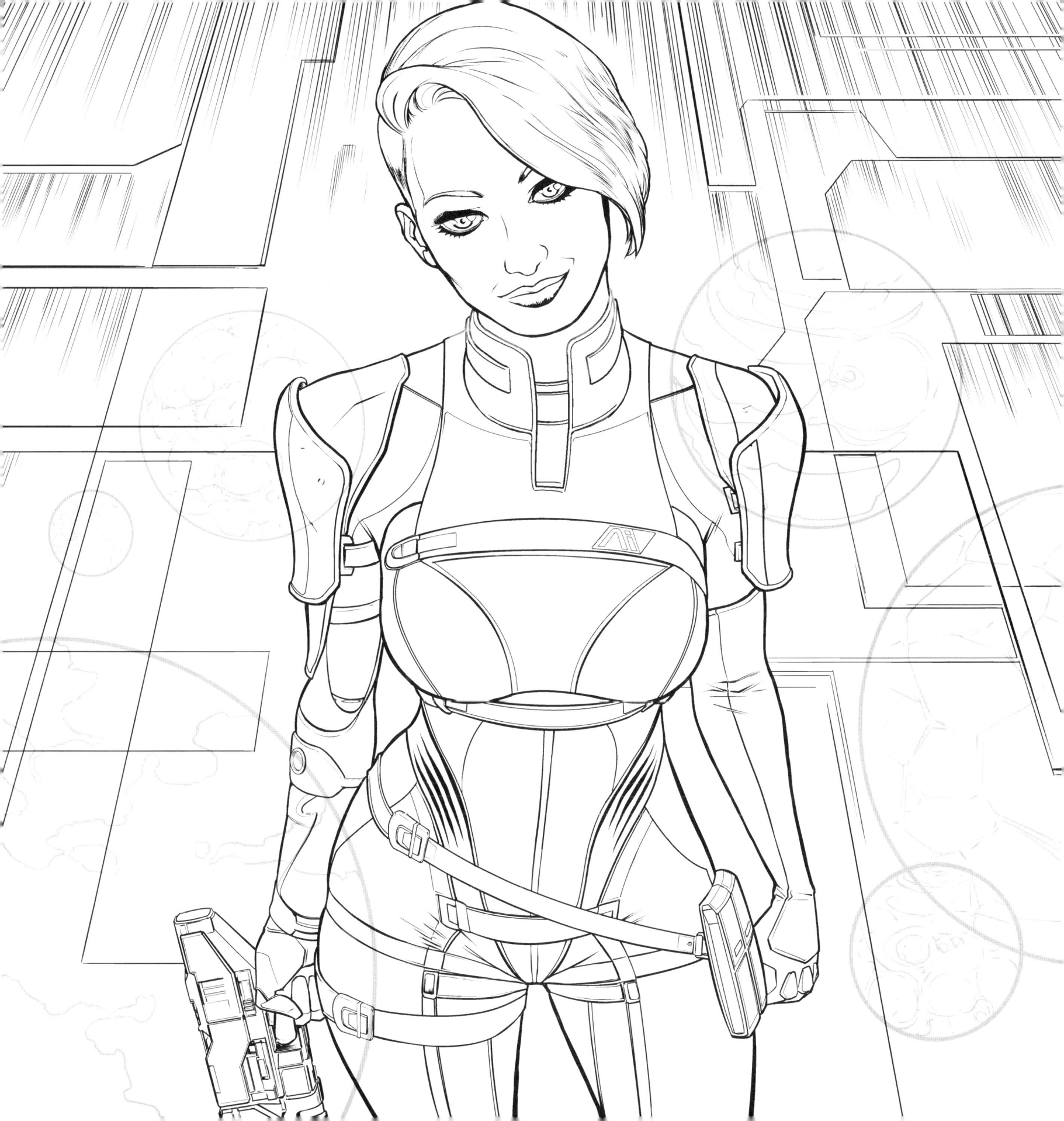

"Your defiance is naive and reckless. This day marks the beginning of your greatness."
—Archon

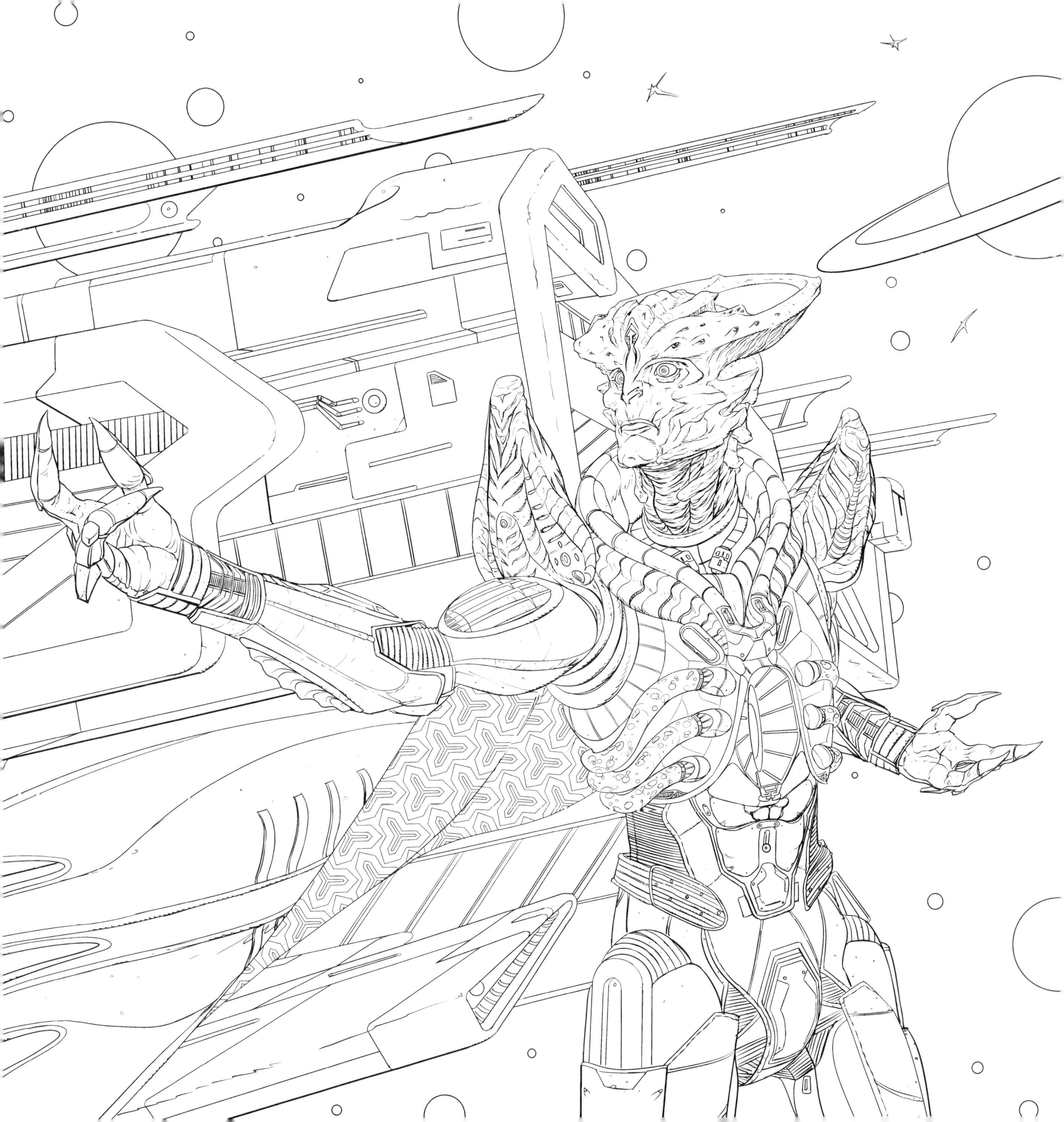

"They call her the *Tempest*."
—Cora Harper

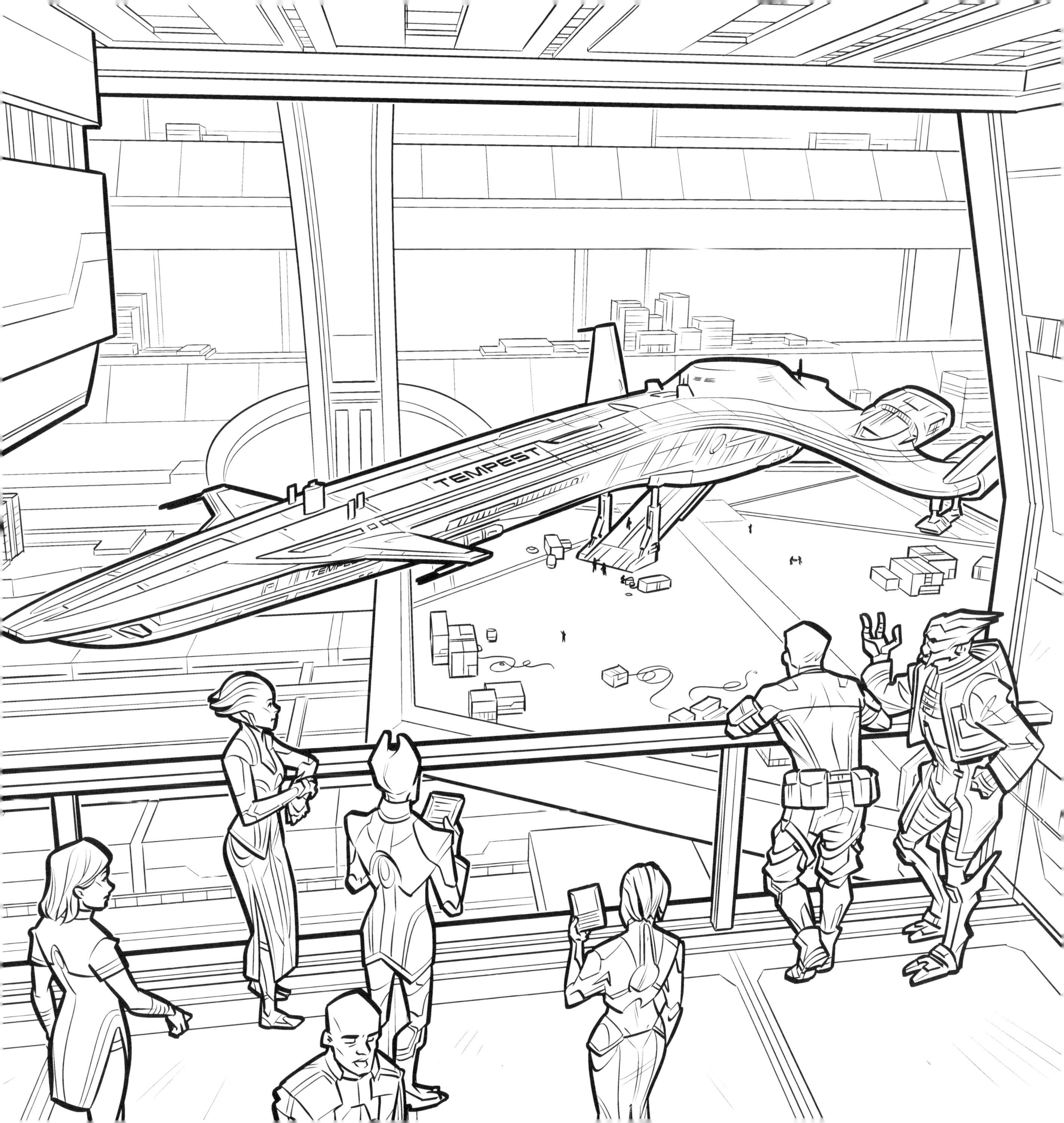
TEMPEST

ABOUT THE ILLUSTRATORS

JUANN CABAL
Juann Cabal was born on a train to Gijón, Spain, in 1986. After graduating from Oviedo School of Art, he worked in advertising for several years, but he felt that he was selling his soul, so he decided to give it all up to turn to his one true passion—comic books. Since then he has worked for Marvel Comics and IDW Publishing. He lives in Oviedo with his wife and two cats. He likes postmodern literature.

RON CHAN
Ron Chan was born and raised in Portland, Oregon and works as a freelance cartoonist, storyboard artist, and illustrator. His comics work has been published by Dark Horse, Marvel, and Image, and he is best known for drawing the *Plants vs. Zombies* comics. His BroShep romanced Jack, and his FemShep romanced Liara. Additionally, he's pretty down with Shakarian. Paragon. Adept. Synthesis. Website: RonChan.net. Twitter, Tumblr, and Instagram: RonDanChan.

GABRIEL GUZMÁN
Argentinean comic book artist Gabriel Guzmán has contributed to various titles including *Lady Death*, *She-Hulk*, *Cable*, *Star Wars*, *Conan*, *Kull*, *Predators*, and most recently, *Father's Day* and *Echoes* with Dark Horse's own Mike Richardson. He currently lives in Viña del Mar, Chile, and works in his studio in front of the Pacific Ocean. See more of his work at GabrielGuzman.Blogspot.com.

ANDRES PONCE
Andres Ponce has worked in the comics field since 2004 as both penciler and inker. He has worked for several American and European companies, such as DC Comics, Image Comics, Titan Publishing, Dynamite Publishing, Avatar Press, Mirage Publishing, IDW, and Dark Horse. His debut in the American market was thanks to the writer Jay Faerber, who gave him the chance to do a short story for his book *Noble Causes*. Later Andres did a miniseries about the Noble family and cocreated with Jay *Firebirds*, a one-shot published for Image Comics. Other credits include such titles and franchises as *Tales of the TMNT*, *Doctor Who*, *Star Wars: The Clone Wars*, *Transformers*, *Transformers Prime*, *War Goddess*, *Dean Koontz's Frankenstein*, *DC Universe vs Masters of the Universe*, and *Bat-Mite*. Currently he is penciling the title *Medic* for Double Take Universe, a book set in the world of the classic movie *Night of the Living Dead*.

MARTÍN TÚNICA
Martín Túnica, born in 1983, is a comic book artist whose work has been published in various countries, including Argentina, the United States, and Italy. He lives in Buenos Aires with his dog, Tesla.

EXPLORE THE *MASS EFFECT* UNIVERSE WITH DARK HORSE!

Created in close collaboration with BioWare and the writers and artists of the games, Dark Horse's *Mass Effect* graphic novels are essential companions to gaming's deepest universe!

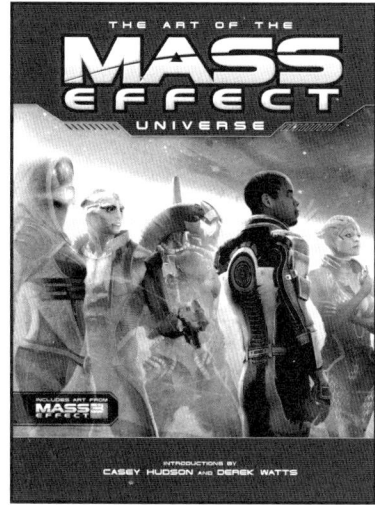

THE ART OF THE MASS EFFECT UNIVERSE
$39.99 | ISBN 978-1-59582-768-5

MASS EFFECT LIBRARY EDITION VOLUME 1
$59.99 | ISBN 978-1-61655-111-7

MASS EFFECT LIBRARY EDITION VOLUME 2
$49.99 | ISBN 978-1-61655-636-5

MASS EFFECT OMNIBUS VOLUME 1
$24.99 | ISBN 978-1-50670-276-6

MASS EFFECT OMNIBUS VOLUME 2
$24.99 | ISBN 978-1-50670-277-3

DarkHorse.com | MassEffect.com

AVAILABLE AT YOUR LOCAL COMICS SHOP OR BOOKSTORE
TO FIND A COMICS SHOP IN YOUR AREA, CALL 1-888-266-4226

© 2017 Electronic Arts Inc. EA and the EA logo are trademarks of Electronic Arts Inc. BioWare, the BioWare logo and Mass Effect are trademarks of EA International (Studio and Publishing) Ltd. Dark Horse Books® and the Dark Horse logo are registered trademarks of Dark Horse Comics, Inc. All rights reserved.